Nola felt her images from together expl like popping corn. **Suddenly her whole body was quivering, and it was all she could do not to lean over and kiss Ramsay, to give in to that impulse and taste and touch that beautiful mouth once again.**

Gripping the underside of the hard plastic chair, she steadied herself. And taking a quick breath, she forced herself to meet his eyes head-on.

"You said you wanted to finish this, Ram, but we can't," she said hoarsely. "Because it never started. It was just a one-night stand, remember?"

"Oh, I remember every single moment of that night. As I'm sure you do, Nola."

His eyes gleamed, and instantly her pulse began to accelerate.

"Only this isn't about just one night anymore. Our one-night stand has had long-term consequences." He gestured toward her stomach.

"But not for you." She looked up at him stubbornly, her blue eyes wide with frustration. "Whatever connection we had, it ended a long time ago."

"Given that you're pregnant with my child, that would seem to be a little premature and counterintuitive," he said softly.

Secret Heirs of Billionaires

There are some things money can't buy...

Living life at lightning pace, these magnates are no strangers to stakes at their highest. It seems they've got it all... That is, until they find out that there's an unplanned item to add to their list of accomplishments!

Achieved:

1. Successful business empire.
2. Beautiful women in their bed.
3. *An heir to bear their name?*

Though every billionaire needs to leave his legacy in safe hands, discovering a secret heir shakes up the carefully orchestrated plan in more ways than one!

Uncover their secrets in:

Look out for more stories in the
Secret Heirs of Billionaires series coming soon!

Louise Fuller

—

KIDNAPPED FOR THE TYCOON'S BABY

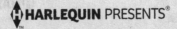

HARLEQUIN PRESENTS®

ISBN-13: 978-0-373-21388-7

Kidnapped for the Tycoon's Baby

First North American publication 2017

Copyright © 2017 by Louise Fuller

HARLEQUIN®
www.Harlequin.com

Printed in U.S.A.

Louise Fuller was a tomboy who hated pink and always wanted to be the prince—not the princess! Now she enjoys creating heroines who aren't pretty pushovers but are strong, believable women. Before writing for Harlequin she studied literature and philosophy at university, and then worked as a reporter for her local newspaper. She lives in Tunbridge Wells with her impossibly handsome husband, Patrick, and their six children.

Books by Louise Fuller

Harlequin Presents

Blackmailed Down the Aisle
Claiming His Wedding Night
A Deal Sealed by Passion
Vows Made in Secret

Visit the Author Profile page at Harlequin.com for more titles.

For Adrian. My brother, and one of the good guys.

CHAPTER ONE

'I'M SORRY ABOUT THIS, Ms Mason. But don't worry.
I'll get you there on time, just like always.'

Feeling the car slow, Nola Mason looked up
from her laptop and frowned, her denim-blue eyes
almost black within the dark interior of the sleek
executive saloon.

Glancing out of the window, she watched a
flatbed truck loaded with cones lumber slowly
through the traffic lights. There had been some
kind of parade in Sydney over the weekend, and
the police and street cleaners were still dealing
with the aftermath.

Thankfully, though, at five o'clock on Monday
morning the traffic was limited to just a few buses
and a handful of cars and, closing her laptop, she
leaned towards her driver.

'I know you will, John. And please don't worry.
I'm just relieved to have you.'

Relieved, and grateful, for not only was John
punctual and polite, he also had near photographic
recall of Sydney's daunting grid of streets.

As the car began to move again she shifted in
her seat. Even after two months of working for
the global tech giant RWI it still felt strange—
fraudulent, even—having a chauffeur-driven limo

at her disposal. She was a cyber architect, not a celebrity! But Ramsay Walker, the company's demanding and maddeningly autocratic CEO, had insisted on it.

Her mouth twisted. It had been the first time she'd objected to something, only to have Ramsay overrule her, but it hadn't been the last. His dictatorial behaviour and her stubborn determination to make a stand had ensured that they clashed fiercely at every subsequent meeting.

But now it was nearly over. Tomorrow was her last day in Sydney and, although, she and her partner Anna were still under contract to troubleshoot any problems in the RWI cyber security framework, they would do so from their office in Edinburgh.

She breathed out softly. And what a relief to finally be free of that intense grey gaze! Only, why then did what she was feeling seem more like regret than relief?

Glancing up at the imposing RWI building, she felt her heart begin beating hard and high in her chest. But right now was *not* the time to indulge in amateur psychology. She was here to work— and, if she was lucky, at this time of the morning she could expect a good two to three hours of uninterrupted access to the security system.

But as she walked past the empty bays in the visitor parking area some of her optimism wilted as she spotted a familiar black Bentley idling in front of the main entrance.

Damn it! She was in no mood for small talk—particularly with the owner of that car—and, ducking her chin, she began to walk faster. But she was not fast enough. Almost as she drew level with the car, the door opened and a man slid out. A woman's voice followed him into the early-morning light, together with the faintest hint of his cologne.

'But, baby, why can't it wait?' she wheedled. 'Come on—we can go back to mine. I'll make it worth your while...'

Unable to stop herself, Nola stole a glance at the man. Predictably, her breath stumbled in her throat and, gritting her teeth, she began to walk faster. She couldn't see his face, but she didn't need to. She would recognise that profile, that languid yet predatory manner anywhere. It was her boss—Ramsay Walker. In that car, at this time of the morning, it was always her boss.

Only the women were different each time.

Ignoring the sudden slick of heat on her skin, she stalked into the foyer. She felt clumsy and stupid, a mix of fear and restlessness and longing churning inside of her. But longing for what?

Working fourteen-hour days, and most weekends, she had no time for romance. And besides, she knew nobody in Sydney except the people in this building, and there was no way she would *ever* have a relationship with a colleague again. Not after what had happened with Connor.

Remembering all the snide glances, and the way people would stop talking when she walked by, she winced inwardly. It had been bad enough that everyone had believed the gossip. What had been so hurtful—so hurtful that she'd still never told anyone, not even her best friend and business partner, Anna—was that it had been Connor who'd betrayed her. Betrayed her and then abandoned her—just like her father had.

It had been humiliating, debilitating, but finally she had understood that love and trust were not necessarily symbiotic or two-way. She'd learnt her lesson, and she certainly wasn't about to forget it for an office fling.

She glanced back to where the woman was still pleading with Ramsay. Gazing at the broad shoulders beneath the crumpled shirt and the tousled surfer hair, Nola felt her heart thudding so loudly she thought one of the huge windows might shatter.

Workplace flings were trouble. But with a man like him it would be trouble squared. Cubed, even.

And anyway her life was too complicated right now for romance. This was the biggest job Cyber Angels had ever taken on, and with Anna away on her honeymoon she was having to manage alone, and do so with a brain and a body that were still struggling to get over three long-haul flights in as many weeks.

Trying to ignore the swell of panic rising inside her, she smiled mechanically at the security guard as he checked her security card. Reaching inside her bag, she pulled out her lift pass—and felt her stomach plummet as it slipped from her fingers and landed on the floor beside a pair of handmade Italian leather loafers.

'Allow me.'

The deep, masculine voice made her scalp freeze. Half turning, she forced a smile onto her face as she took the card from the man's outstretched hand.

'Thank you.'

'My pleasure.'

Turning, she walked quickly towards the lift, her skin tightening with irritation and a sort of feverish apprehension, as Ramsay Walker strolled alongside her, his long strides making it easy for him to keep pace.

As the lift doors opened it was on the tip of her tongue to tell him that she would use the stairs. But, given that her office was on the twenty-first floor, she knew it would simply make her look churlish or—worse—as though she cared about sharing the lift with him.

'Early start!'

Her skin twitched in an involuntary response to his languid East Coast accent, and she allowed herself a brief glance at his face. Instantly she regretted it. His dark grey eyes were watching her casually…a lazy smile tugged at his beautiful mouth. A mouth that had been kissing her all over every night since she'd first met him—but only in her dreams.

Trying to subdue the heat of her thoughts, praying that her face showed nothing of their content, she shrugged stiffly. 'I'm a morning person.'

'Is that right?' he drawled. 'I like the night-time myself.'

Night-time. The words whispered inside her head and she felt her body react to the darkness and danger it implied, her pulse slowing, goosebumps prickling over her skin. Only how was it possible to create such havoc with just a handful of syllables? she thought frantically.

'Really?' Trying her hardest to ignore the strange tension throbbing between them, she forced her expression into what she hoped looked like boredom and, glancing away, stared straight ahead. 'And yet here you are.'

She felt his gaze on the side of her face.

'Well, I got waylaid at a party…'

Remembering the redhead in the car, she felt a sharp nip of jealousy as stifling a yawn, he stretched his arms back behind his shoulders, the gesture somehow implying more clearly than words exactly what form that waylaying had taken.

'It seemed simpler to come straight to work. I take it you weren't out partying?'

His voice was soft, and yet it seemed to hook beneath her skin so that suddenly she had no option but to look up at him.

'Not my scene. I need my sleep,' she said crisply.

She knew she sounded prudish. But better that than to give this man even a hint of encouragement. Not that he needed any—he clearly believed himself to be irresistible. And, judging by his hit rate with women, he was right.

He laughed softly. 'You need to relax. Clio has a party most weekends. You should come along next time.'

'Surely that would be up to Clio?' she said primly, and he smiled—a curling, mocking smile that made the hairs on the back of her neck stand up.

His eyes glittered. 'If I'm happy, she's happy.'

She gritted her teeth. Judging by the photos of supermodels with tear-stained faces, papped leaving his apartment, that clearly wasn't true. Not that it was any of her business, she thought quickly as the lift stopped.

There was a short hiss as the doors opened, and then, turning to face him, Nola lifted her chin.

'Thank you, but no. I never socialise with people at work. In my opinion, the disadvantages out-weigh the benefits.'

His eyes inspected her lazily. 'Then maybe you should let me change your opinion. I can be very persuasive.'

Her stomach dipped, and something treacher-ously soft and warm slipped over her skin as his grey gaze rested on her face. When he looked at her like that it was hard not to feel persuaded.

She drew a breath. Hard, but not impossible.

'I don't doubt that. Unfortunately, though, I al-ways put workplace considerations above every-thing else.'

And before he had a chance to respond she slipped through the doors, just before they slid shut.

Her heart was racing. Her legs felt weak. Any woman would have been tempted by such an in-vitation. But she had been telling the truth.

Since her disastrous relationship with Connor, she had made a decision and stuck to it. Her work life and her personal life were two separate, con-current strands, and she never mixed the two. She would certainly never date anyone from work. Or go to a party with them.

Particularly if the invitation came from her boss.

Remembering the way his eyes had drifted ap-praisingly over her face, she shivered.

And most especially not if that boss was Ramsay Walker.

In business, he was heralded as a genius, and he was undeniably handsome and sexy. But Ramsay Walker was the definition of trouble.

Okay, she knew with absolute certainty that sex with him would be mind-blowing. How could it not be? The man was a force of nature made flesh and blood—the human personification of a hurricane or a tsunami. But that was why he was so dangerous. He might be powerful, intense, unstoppable, but he also left chaos and destruction behind him.

Even if she didn't believe all the stories in the media about his womanising, she had witnessed it with her own eyes. Ramsay clearly valued novelty and variety above all else. And, if that wasn't enough of a warning to stay well away, he'd also publicly and repeatedly stated his desire never to marry or have children.

Not that she was planning on doing either any time soon. She and her mother had done fine on their own, but getting involved on any level with a man who seemed so determinedly opposed to such basic human connections just wasn't an option. It had taken too long to restore her pride and build up a good reputation, to throw either away for a heartbreaking smile.

Three hours later, though, she was struggling to defend both.

* * *

In the RWI boardroom silence had fallen as the man at the head of the table leaned back in his chair, his casual stance at odds with the dark intensity of his gaze. A gaze that was currently locked on Nola's face.

'So let me get this right,' he observed softly. 'What you're trying to say is that I'm being naive. Or complacent.'

A pulse of anger leapfrogged over his skin.

Did she *really* think she was going to get away with insulting him in his own boardroom? Ram thought, watching Nola blink, seeing anger, confusion and frustration colliding in those blue, blue eyes.

Eyes that made a man want to quench his thirst—and not for water. The same blue eyes that should have warned him to ignore her CV and glowing references and stick with men in grey suits who talked about algorithms and crypto-ransomware. But Nola Mason was not the kind of woman it was easy to ignore.

Refusing his invitation to meet at the office, she had insisted instead that they meet in some grimy café in downtown Sydney.

There, surrounded by surly teenagers in hoodies and bearded geeks, she had shown him just how easy it was to breach RWI's security. It had been an impressive display—unorthodox, but credible and provocative.

Only not as provocative as the sight of her long slim legs and rounded bottom in tight black jeans, or the strip of smooth bare stomach beneath her T-shirt that he'd glimpsed when she reached over to the next table for a napkin.

It wasn't love at first sight.

For starters, he didn't believe in love.

Only, watching her talk, he had been knocked sideways by lust, by curiosity, by the challenge in those blue eyes. By whatever it was that triggered sexual attraction between two people. It had been beyond his conscious control, and he'd had to struggle not to pull her across the table by the long dark hair spilling onto the shoulders of her battered leather jacket.

But it was the dark blue velvet ribbon tied around her throat that had goaded his senses to the point where he had thought he was going to black out.

Those eyes, that choker, had made up his mind. In other words, he'd let his libido hire her.

It was the first time he'd ever allowed lust to dictate a business decision. And it would be the last, he thought grimly, glancing once again at the tersely written email she had sent him that morning. He gritted his teeth. If Ms Nola Mason was expecting him to pay more, she could damn well sing for it.

Nola swallowed, shifting in her seat. Her heart was pounding, and she was struggling to stay calm beneath the battleship-grey of Ram's scrutiny. Most CEOs were exacting and autocratic, but cyber security was typically an area in which the boss was almost always willing to hand over leadership to an expert.

Only Ram was not a typical boss.

Right from that first interview it had been clear that not only was his reputation as the *enfant terrible* of the tech industry fully justified, but that, unusually, he could also demonstrate considerably more than a working knowledge of the latest big data technologies.

Truthfully, however, Ram's intelligence wasn't the only reason she found it so hard to confront him. His beauty, his innate self-confidence, and that still focus—the sense that he was watching her and only her—made her heart flip-flop against her ribs.

Her blue eyes flickered across the boardroom table to where he sat, lounging opposite her. It might be shallow, but who wouldn't be affected by such blatant perfection? And it didn't help that he appealed on so many different levels.

With grey eyes that seemed to lighten and darken in harmony with his moods, messy black hair, a straight nose, and a jaw permanently darkened with stubble, he might just as easily be a poet or a revolutionary as a CEO. And the hard definition of muscle beneath his gleaming white shirt only seemed to emphasise that contradiction even more.

Dragging her gaze back up to his face, Nola felt her nerves ball painfully. The tension in his jaw told her that she was balancing on eggshells. *Concentrate*, she told herself—surely she hadn't meant to imply that he was naive or complacent?

'No, that's not what I'm saying,' she said quickly, ignoring the faint sigh of relief that echoed round the table as she did so. She drew in a deep breath. 'What you're actually being is arrogant, and unreasonable.'

Somebody—she wasn't sure who—gave a small whimper.

For a fraction of a second Ram thought he might have misheard her. Nobody called him arrogant or unreasonable. But, glancing across at Nola, he knew immediately that he'd heard her correctly.

Her cheeks were flushed, but she was eyeing him steadily, and he felt a flicker of anger and something like admiration. She was brave—he'd give her that. And determined. He knew his reputation, and it had been well and truly earned. His negotiating skills were legendary, and his single-minded ruthlessness had turned a loan from his grandfather into a global brand.

A pulse began to beat in his groin. Normally she would be emptying her desk by now. Only the humming in his blood seemed to block out all rational thought so that he felt dazed, disorientated by her accusation. But why? What was it about this woman that made it so difficult for him to stay focused?

He didn't know. But whatever it was it had been instant and undeniable. When he'd walked into that coffee shop she had stood up, shaken his hand, and his body had reacted automatically—not just a spark but a fire starting in his blood and burning through his veins.

It had been devastating, unprecedented. At the time he'd assumed it was because she was so unlike any of the other women of his acquaintance. Women who would sacrifice anything and *anyone* to fit in, to make their lives smooth. Women who chose conformity and comfort over risk.

Nola took risks. That was obvious from the way she had dressed and behaved at her interview. He liked it that she broke the rules. Every single time he came into contact with her he liked it more—liked *her* more.

And she liked him too.

Only every single time she came into contact with him she gave him the brush-off. Or at least she tried too. But her eyes gave her away.

As though sensing his thoughts, Nola glanced up and looked away, her hand rising protectively to touch her throat. Instantly the pulse in his groin began to beat harder and faster.

He had never had to chase a woman before—let alone coax her into his bed. It was both maddening and unbelievably erotic.

At the thought of Nola in his bed, wearing nothing but that velvet choker, he felt a stab of sexual frustration so painful that he had to grip the arms of his chair to stop himself from groaning out loud.

'That's a pretty damning assessment, Ms Mason,' he said softly. 'Obviously if I thought you were being serious we'd be having a very different conversation. So I'm going to assume you're trying to shock me into changing my mind.'

Nola took a breath. Her insides felt tight and a prickling heat was spreading up her spine. Could everyone else in the room feel the tension between her and Ram? Or was it all in her head?

Stupid question. She knew it was real—and not just real. It was dangerous. Whatever this thing was between them, it was clearly hazardous—not only to her reason but to her instinct for self-preservation. Why else was she picking a fight with the boss in public?

Abruptly he leaned forward, and as their eyes met she shivered. His gaze was so intent that suddenly it felt as though they were alone, facing each other like two Western gunslingers in a saloon bar.

'Nice try! But I'm not that sensitive.'

Without warning the intensity faded from his handsome features and, glancing swiftly round the room, she knew her anger must look out of place—petulant, even. No doubt that had been his intention all along: to make her look emotional and unprofessional.

Gritting her teeth, she leaned back in her chair, trying to match his nonchalance.

Watching her fingers curl into a fist around her pen, Ram smiled slowly. 'I don't know whether to be disappointed or impressed by you, Ms Mason. It usually takes people a lot less than two months to realise I'm arrogant and unreasonable. However, they don't tend to say it to my face. Either way, though, I'm not inclined to change my mind. Or permit you to change yours. You see, I only have one thousand four hundred and forty minutes in any day, and I don't like to waste them on ill-thought-out negotiations like this one.'

Watching the flush of colour spread over her pale skin, he felt a stab of satisfaction. She had got under his skin; now he had not got under hers, And he was going to make sure it stung.

'I gave you a budget—a very generous budget—and I see no reason to increase it on the basis of some whim.'

Nola glared at him. 'This is not a whim, Mr Walker. It is a response to your email informing me that the software launch date has been brought forward by six weeks.'

Had he stuck to the original deadline, the new system would have been up and running for several months prior to the launch, giving her ample time to iron out any glitches. Now, though, the team she'd hired and trained for RWI would have to work longer hours to run all the necessary checks, and overtime meant more money.

Ram leaned forward. 'I run a business—a very successful one—that is currently paying your salary, and part of that success comes from knowing my market inside out. And this software needs to be on sale as soon as possible. And by "as soon as possible" I mean *now*.'

She blinked trying to break the spell of his eyes on hers and the small taunting smile on his lips.

Taking a breath, she steadied herself. 'I understand that. But *now* changes things. *Now* is expensive. But not nearly as expensive as it will be when your system gets hacked.'

'That sounds awfully like a threat, Ms Mason.'

She took another quick breath, her hand lifting instinctively to her throat. Feeling the blood pulsing beneath her fingertips, she straightened her spine.

'That's because it is. But better that it comes from me than them. Hackers break the rules, which means *I* have to break the rules. The difference is that I'm not about to steal or destroy or publicise your data. Nor am I going to extort money from you.'

'Not true.' The corner of his mouth lifted, as though she had made a joke, but there was no laughter in his eyes. 'Okay, you don't sneak in through the back door. You just give me one of those butter-wouldn't-melt-in-your-mouth smiles and put an invoice on my desk!'

'I can protect your company, Mr Walker. But I can't do that if my hands are tied behind my back.'

He tilted his head, his expression shifting, his dark gaze locking onto her face. 'Of course not. But, personally, I never let anyone tie me up unless we've decided on a safe word beforehand. Maybe you should do the same.'

There was some nervous laughter around the table. But before she could respond, he twisted in his seat and gestured vaguely towards the door.

'I need to have a private conversation with Ms Mason.'

Stomach churning, Nola watched as the men and women filed silently out of the room. Finally the door closed with a quiet click and she felt a ripple of apprehension slither over her skin as she waited for him to speak.

But he didn't say anything. Instead he simply stared out of the window at the blue sky, his face calm and untroubled.

Her heartbeat accelerated. *Damn him!* She knew he was making her wait, proving his power. If only she could tell him where to put his job. But this contract was not only paying her and Anna's wages, RWI was a global brand—a household name—and getting a good reference would propel their company, Cyber Angels, into the big time.

So, willing herself to stay cool-headed, she sat as the silence spread to the four corners of the room. Finally he pushed back his seat and stood up. Her pulse twitched in her throat as she watched him walk slowly around the table and come to a halt in front of her.

'You're costing me a great deal of money already. And now you're about to cost me a whole lot more.' He stared at her coolly. 'Are you sure there's nothing else you'd like, Nola? This table, perhaps? My car? Maybe the shirt off my back?'

He was looking for her to react. Which meant she should stay silent and seated. But it was the first time he had said her name, and hearing it spoken in that soft, sexy drawl caught her off guard.

She jerked to her feet, her body acting independently, tasting the sharp tang of adrenaline in her mouth.

Instantly she knew she'd made a mistake. She was close enough to reach out and touch that beautifully shaped mouth. In other words, too close. *Walk away*, she shouted silently. *Better still, run!*

But for some reason her legs wouldn't do what her brain was suggesting.

Instead, she glowered at him, her blue eyes darkening with anger. 'Yes, that's right, Mr Walker. That's exactly what I want. The shirt off your back.'

But it wasn't. What she really wanted was to turn the tables. Goad him into losing control. Make him feel this same conflicted, confusing mass of fear and frustration and desire.

His fingers were hovering over the top button of his shirt, his eyes holding hers. 'You're sure about that?' he said softly.

The menacing undertone beneath the softness cut through her emotion and brought her to her senses.

At the other end of a table, surrounded by people, Ram Walker was disturbing, distracting. But up close and unchaperoned he was formidable.

And she was out of her depth.

Breathing in sharply, she shook her head, her pulse quickening with helpless anger as he gave her a small satisfied smile.

'And I thought you liked breaking the rules.'

His eyes gleamed and she knew he was goading her again, but she didn't care. Right now all she wanted was to be somewhere far away from this man who seemed to have the power to turn her inside out and off balance.

'Is there anything else you'd like to discuss?' he asked with an exaggerated politeness that seemed designed to test her self-control.

He waited until she shook her head, and then, turning, he walked towards the door.

'I'll speak to the accountants today.'

It was with relief bordering on delirium that she watched him leave the room.

Back in her office, she sat down behind her desk and let out a jagged breath.

Her hands were trembling and she felt hot and dizzy.

Leaning back in her chair, she picked up her notebook and a pencil. She knew it was anachronistic for a techie like herself to use pen and paper, but her mother had always used a notebook. Besides, it helped her clear her mind and unwind— and right now, with Ram Walker's goading words running on a loop round her head, she needed all the help she could get.

But she had barely flipped open her notebook when her phone buzzed. She hesitated before picking it up. If it was Ram, she was going to let it ring out. Her nerves were still jangling from their last encounter, and she couldn't face another head-to-head right now. But glancing at the screen, she felt a warm rush of happiness.

It was Anna.

A chat with her best friend would be the perfect antidote to that showdown with Ram.

'Hey, I wasn't expecting to hear from you. Why are you calling me? This is your honeymoon. Shouldn't you be gazing into Robbie's eyes, or writhing about with him on some idyllic beach?'

Hearing Anna's snort of laughter, she realised just how much she was missing her easy-going friend and business partner.

'I promise you, sex on the beach is overrated! Sand gets everywhere. And I mean *everywhere*.'

'Okay, too much information, Mrs Harris.' She began to doodle at the edges of the paper.

'Oh, Noles, you have no idea how weird it is to be Mrs Somebody, let alone Mrs Harris.'

'No idea at all! And planning to stay that way,' she said lightly.

Marriage had never been high on her to-do list. She was happy for Anna, of course. But her parents' divorce had left her wary of making vows and promises. And her disastrous relationship with Connor had only reinforced her instinctive distrust of the sort of trust and intimacy that marriage required.

Anna giggled. 'Every time anyone calls me that I keep thinking my mother-in-law's here. It's terrifying!'

She and Nola both burst out laughing.

'So why are you ringing me?' Nola said finally, when she could speak again.

'Well, we were at the pool, and Robbie got talking to this guy, and guess what? He's a neurosurgeon too. So you can imagine what happened next.'

Nola nodded. Anna's husband had recently been appointed as a consultant at one of Edinburgh's top teaching hospitals. He was as passionate about his work as he was about his new wife.

'Anyway, I left them yapping on about central core function and some new scanner, and that made me think of you, slogging away in Sydney all on your own. So I thought I'd give you a call and see how everything's going...'

Tucking the phone against her shoulder, Nola rolled her eyes. 'Everything's fine. There was a bit of a problem this morning, but nothing I couldn't handle.'

She paused, felt a betraying flush of colour spreading over her cheeks, and was grateful that Anna was on the end of a phone and not in the same room.

There was a short silence. Then, 'So, you and Ramsay Walker are getting on okay?'

Nola frowned.

'Yes...' She hesitated. 'Well, no. Not really. It's complicated. But it's okay,' she said quickly, as

Anna made a noise somewhere between a wail and groan.

'I knew I should have postponed the honeymoon! Please tell me you haven't done anything stupid.'

Nola swallowed. She had—but thankfully only in the safe zone of her imagination.

'We had a few words about the budget, but I handled it and it's fine. I promise.'

'That's good.' She heard Anna breathe out. 'Look, Noles, I know you think he's arrogant and demanding—'

'It's not a matter of opinion, Anna. It's a fact. He *is* arrogant and demanding.'

And spoiled. How could he not be? He was the only son and heir to a fortune; his every whim had probably been indulged from birth. He might like to boast that he said no to almost everything, but she was willing to bet an entire year's salary that nobody had ever said no to him.

'I know,' her friend said soothingly. 'But for the next twenty-four hours he's still the boss. And if we get a good reference from him we'll basically be able to print money. We might even be able to pay off our loan.' She giggled. 'Besides, you have to admit that there are *some* perks working for him.'

'Anna Harris, you're a married woman. You shouldn't be having thoughts like that.'

'Why not? I love my Robbie, but Ram Walker is *gorgeous*.'

Laughing reluctantly, Nola shook her head. 'He is so not your type, Anna.'

'If you believe that you must have been looking too long into that big old Australian sun! He's *every* woman's type. As long as they're breathing.'

Opening her mouth, wanting to disagree, to deny what she knew to be true, Nola glanced down at her notepad, at the sketch she had made of Ram.

Who was she trying to kid?

'Fine. He's gorgeous. Happy now?'

But as she swung round in her seat her words froze on her lips, and Anna's response was lost beneath the sudden deafening beat of her heart.

Lounging in the open doorway, his muscular body draped against the frame, Ram Walker was watching her with a mocking gaze that told her he had clearly heard her last remark.

There was no choice but to front it out. Acknowledging his presence with a small, tight smile, she closed her notebook carefully and, as casually as she could manage, said, 'Okay, that all sounds fine. Send the data over as soon as possible and I'll take a look at it.'

Ignoring Anna's confused reply, she hung up. Her heart was ricocheting against her ribs.

'Mr Walker. How can I help you?'

He stared at her calmly, his grey eyes holding her captive.

'Let's not worry about that now,' he said easily. 'Why don't we talk about how I can help *you*?'

She stared at him in silence. Where was this conversation going?

'I don't understand—*you* want to help *me*?'

'Of course. You're only with us one more day, and I want to make that time as productive as possible. Which is why I want you to have dinner with me this evening.'

'You mean tonight?'

Her voice sounded too high, and she felt her cheeks grow hot as he raised an eyebrow.

'Well, it can't be any other night,' he said slowly. 'You're flying home tomorrow, aren't you?'

Nola licked her lips nervously, a dizzying heat sliding over her skin. Dinner with her billionaire boss might sound like a dream date, but frankly it was a risk she wasn't prepared to take.

'That would be lovely. Obviously,' she lied. 'But I've got a couple of meetings, and the one with the tactical team at five will probably overrun.'

He locked eyes with her.

'Oh, don't worry. I cancelled it.'

She gazed at him in disbelief, and then a ripple of anger flickered over her skin.

'You cancelled it?'

He nodded. 'It seemed easier. So is seven-thirty okay?'

'Okay?' she spluttered. 'No, it's *not* okay. You can't just march in and cancel my meetings for a dinner date.'

He raised an eyebrow and took a step backwards. 'Date? Is that why you're so flustered? I'm sorry to disappoint you, Ms Mason, but I'm afraid we won't be alone.'

His words made her heart hammer against her chest, and a hot flush of embarrassment swept across her face. She was suddenly so angry she wanted to scream.

'I don't want to be alone with you,' she snapped, her hands curling into fists. 'Why would I want that?'

He smiled at her mockingly. 'I suppose for the same reason as any other woman in your position. Sadly, though, I've invited some people I think you should meet. They'll be good for your business.'

She stared at him mutely, unable to think of anything to say that wouldn't result in her being fired on the spot.

His gaze shifted from her face to her fists, grey eyes gleaming like polished pewter.

'Nothing else to say? You disappoint me, Ms Mason! I was hoping for at least one devastating comeback. Okay, I'll pick you up from your hotel later. Be ready. And don't worry about thanking me now. You can do that later too.'

'But I've got to pack!' she called after him, the bottleneck of words in her throat finally bursting.

But it was too late. He'd gone.

Staring after him, Nola felt a trickle of fury run down her spine. *Any other woman in your position.* How dared he lump her in with all his other wannabe conquests? He was impossible, overbearing and conceited.

But as a hot, swift shiver ran through her body she swore under her breath, for if that was true then why did he still affect her in this way?

Well, it was going to stop now.

Standing up, she stormed across her office and slammed the door.

Breathing out hard, she stared at her shaking hands. It felt good to give way to frustration and anger. But closing a door was easy. She had a horrible feeling that keeping Ram Walker out of her head, even when she was back in Scotland, was going to be a whole lot harder.

CHAPTER TWO

FROM HIS OFFICE on the twenty-second floor, Ram stared steadily out of the window at the Pacific Ocean. The calm expression on his face in no way reflected the turmoil inside his head.

Something was wrong. He looked down at the file he was supposed to be reading and frowned. For starters, he was sleeping badly, and he had a near permanent headache. But worst of all he was suffering from a frustrating and completely uncharacteristic inability to focus on what was important to him. His business.

Or it had been important to him right up until the moment he'd walked into that backstreet café and met Nola Mason.

A prickling tension slid down his spine and his chest squeezed tighter.

Down in the bay, a yacht cut smoothly through the waves. But for once his eyes didn't follow its progress. Instead it was the clear, sparkling blue of the water that drew his gaze.

His jaw tightened, pulling the skin across the high curves of his cheekbones.

Two months ago his life had been perfect. But one particular woman, whose eyes were the exact shade as the ocean, had turned that life upside down.

Nola.

He ran the syllables slowly over his tongue. Before he'd met her the name had simply been an acronym for New Orleans—or the Big Easy, as it was also known. His eyes narrowed. But any connection between Nola Mason and the city straddling the Mississippi ended there. Nola might be many things—sexy, smart and seriously good at her job. But she wasn't easy. In fact she was unique among women in that she seemed utterly impervious to his charms.

Thinking back to their conversation in the boardroom, remembering the way she had stood up to him in front of the directors, he felt the same mix of frustration, admiration and desire that seemed to define every single contact he had with her.

It was a mix of feelings that was entirely new to him.

Normally women tripped over themselves to please him. They certainly never kept him at arm's length, or spouted 'workplace considerations' as a reason for turning him down.

Turning him down! Even just thinking the words inside his head made him see every shade of red. Nobody had ever turned him down—in the boardroom *or* the bedroom.

He glanced down at the unread report, but there was no place to hide from the truth: despite the fact that his instincts were screaming at him to keep his distance, he couldn't stop thinking about Nola and her refusal to sleep with him. Her stupid, logical, perfectly justified refusal to break the rules. *Her* rules.

He closed the file with a snap. His rules too.

And that was what was really driving him crazy. The fact that up until a couple of months ago he would have agreed with her. Workplace relationships were a poisoned chalice. They caused tension and upset. And not once had he ever been tempted to break those rules and sleep with an employee.

Only Nola Mason was not just a temptation.

She was a virus in his blood.

No. His mouth twisted. She was more like malware in his system, stealthily undermining his strength, his stability, his sanity.

But there was a cure.

His groin hardened.

He knew what it was, and so did she.

He'd seen it in the antagonism flickering in those blue eyes, heard it in the huskiness of her voice. And her resistance, her refusal to acknowledge it was merely fuelling his desire. His anticipation of the moment when finally she surrendered to him.

He tossed the file onto his desk, feeling a pulsing, breathless excitement scrabbling up inside him.

Of course, being Nola, she would offer a truce, not a surrender. Those eyes, that mouth, might suggest an uninhibited sensuality, but he sensed that the determined slant of her chin was not just a pose adopted for business but a reflection of how she behaved out of work and in bed.

Picturing Nola, her blue eyes narrowing into fierce slits as she straddled his naked body, he felt his spine melt into his chair. But truces could only happen if both parties came to the table—which was why he'd invited her to dinner. Not an intimate, candlelit tryst. He knew Nola, and she would have instantly rejected anything so blatant. But now she knew it was to be a business dinner at a crowded restaurant, she would relax—hell, they might even end up sharing a dessert.

His mouth curved up into a satisfied smile. Or, better still, they could save dessert until they got back to his penthouse.

So this was what it felt like to be famous, Nola thought as she walked self-consciously between the tables in the exclusive restaurant Ram had chosen. It was certainly an experience, although she wasn't sure it was one she'd ever want to repeat.

The Wool Shed was the hottest dining ticket in town, but even though it was midweek, and the award-winning restaurant was packed, to her astonishment Ram hadn't bothered to book. For any normal person that would have meant looking for somewhere else to eat. Clearly those rules didn't apply to Ram Walker, for now, within seconds of his arrival, the maître d' was leading them to a table with a view across the bay to the Opera House.

'I think I may have told our guests that dinner was at eight, so it's going to be just the two of us for a bit. Sorry about that.'

Nola stared at him warily. He didn't sound sorry; he sounded completely unrepentant. Meeting his gaze, she saw that he didn't look sorry either. In fact, he seemed to be enjoying the uneasiness that was clearly written all over her face.

Sliding into the seat he'd pulled out, Nola breathed out carefully. 'That's fine. It'll give you a chance to brief me on our mystery guests.'

She felt him smile behind her. 'Of course—and don't worry, your chaperones will arrive very soon. I promise.'

Gritting her teeth, she watched him drop gracefully into the chair beside her. At work it had been easy to tell herself that the tension between them was just some kind of personality clash or a battle of wills. Now, though, she could see that ever since she'd met Ram that first time, the battle had been raging inside her.

A battle between her brain and her body...between common sense and her basest carnal urges. And, much as she would have liked to deny it, or pretend it wasn't true, the sexual pull between them was as real and tangible as the bottles of still and sparkling water on the table. So much so that only by pressing her fingers into the armrests of her chair could she stop herself from reaching out to touch the smooth curve of his jaw.

Her hand twitched. It was like trying to ignore a mosquito bite. The urge to scratch was overwhelming.

But surely walking into this restaurant with him was just what she'd needed to remind her why it was best not to give in to that urge—for Ram wasn't just her boss. He was way out of her league.

In a room filled with beautiful people, he was the unashamed focus of every eye. As he'd strolled casually to their table conversations had dwindled and even the waiters had seemed to freeze; it had been as though everyone in the restaurant had taken a sort of communal breath.

And it was easy to see why.

Glancing up, she felt a jolt of hunger spike inside her.

There was something about him that commanded attention. Of course he looked amazing— each feature, from his long dark eyelashes to the tiny scar on his cheekbone, looked as though it had been lovingly executed by an artist. But it wasn't just his dark, sculpted looks that tugged at the senses. He had a quality of certainty that was unique, compelling, irresistible.

He was the ultimate cool boy at school, she

decided. And now he was sitting next to her, his arm resting casually over the back of her chair, the scent of his cologne making a dizzy heat spread over her skin.

Unable to stop herself, she glanced sideways and felt her breath catch in her throat.

He was just too ridiculously beautiful.

As though sensing her focus, he turned, and the air was punched out of her lungs as his dark grey gaze scanned her face.

'What's the matter?'

'Nothing,' she lied. 'Are you going to tell me who we're meeting?' She tried to arrange her expression into that same mix of casual and professional that he projected so effortlessly. 'Are they local?'

'They're a little bigger than just Australia. It's Craig Aldin and Will Fraser. They own—'

'A&F Freight,' she finished his sentence. 'That's the—'

'The biggest logistics company in the southern hemisphere.'

His eyes glittered as he in turn finished *her* sentence, a hint of a smile tugging at his mouth. 'Maybe we should try ordering dinner this way. It would be like a new game: gastronomic consequences.'

She tried not to respond to that smile, but it was like trying to resist gravity.

'It could be fun,' she said cautiously. 'Although we might end up with some challenging flavour combinations.'

His eyes didn't leave her face. 'Well, I've never been that vanilla in my tastes,' he said softly.

Her heart banged against her ribs like a bird hitting a window. There it was again—that spark of danger and desire, her flint striking his steel.

But as he picked up the water bottle and filled her glass she bit her lip, felt a knot forming in her stomach. Flirting with Ram in this crowded restaurant might feel safe. Playing with fire, however, was never a good idea—and especially not with a man who was as experienced and careless with women as he was.

She needed to remember that the next time he made her breath jerk in her throat, but right now she needed to dampen that flame and steer the conversation back to work.

'Is A&F looking to upgrade its system?' she asked quickly, ignoring the mocking gleam in his eyes.

Ram stared at her for a moment and then shrugged.

It was the same every time. Back and forth. Gaining her trust, then losing it again. Like trying to stroke a feral cat. Just as he thought he was close enough to touch, she'd retreat. It was driving him mad.

He shifted in his seat, wishing he could shift the ache inside his body. If he couldn't persuade her to relax soon he was going to do himself some permanent damage.

His eyes drifted lazily over her body. In that cream blouse, dark skirt and stockings, and with those blue eyes watching him warily across the table, she looked more like a sleek Siamese than the feisty street cat she'd been channelling in their meeting that morning.

'Yes—and soon. That's why I want you to meet with them today.'

As he put the bottle back on the table his hand brushed against hers, and suddenly she was struggling to remember what he'd just said, let alone figure out how to reply.

'Thank you,' she said finally.

His expression was neutral. 'Of course it might mean coming back to Australia.'

Frowning, she looked into his face. 'That won't be a problem.'

'Really? It's just that you live on the other side of the world. I thought you might have somebody missing you. Someone significant.'

Nola blinked. How had they ended up talking about this? About her private life.

Ram Walker was too damn sharp for his own good. He made connections that were barely visible while she was still struggling to join the dots.

His gaze was so intense that suddenly she wanted to lift her hand and shield her face. But instead she thought about her flat, with its high ceilings and shabby old sofas. It was her home, and she loved it, but it wasn't a *somebody*. Truthfully, there hadn't been anyone in her life since Connor.

Her throat tightened. Connor—with his sweet face and his floppy hair. And his desire to be liked. A desire that had meant betraying her trust in the most humiliating way possible. He hadn't quite matched up to her father's level of unreliability, but then, he'd only been in her life a matter of months.

Of course since their break-up she hadn't taken a vow of celibacy. She'd gone out with a couple of men on more than a couple of dates and they'd been pleasant enough. But none had been memorable, and right now the only significant living thing in her flat was a cactus called Colin.

She shook her head. 'No,' she said at last. 'Anna's the home bird. I've no desire to tie myself down any time soon. I like my independence too much.'

Ram nodded. Letting his gaze wander over her face, he took in the flushed cheeks and the dilated pupils and felt a tug down low in his stomach. A pulse of heat flickered beneath his skin.

Independence. The word tasted sweet and dark

and glossy in his mouth—like a cherry bursting against his tongue. At that moment, had he believed in soulmates, he would have thought he'd found his. For here was a woman who was not afraid to be herself. To stand alone in the world.

His heart was pounding. He wanted her more than he'd ever wanted anyone—anything. If only he could reach over and pull her against him, strip her naked and take her right here, right now—

But instead a waiter brought over some bread and, grateful for the nudge back to reality, Ram leaned back in his chair, trying to school his thoughts, his breathing, his body, into some sort of order.

'She's impressive, your partner,' he said, when finally the waiter left them alone.

He watched her face soften, the blue eyes widen with affection, and suddenly he wondered how it would feel to be the object of that incredible gaze. For someone to care that much about him.

The idea made him feel strangely vulnerable and, picking up his glass, he downed his water so that it hit his stomach with a thump.

She nodded eagerly. 'She was always top of the class.'

He nodded. 'I can believe that. But I wasn't talking about her tech skills. It's her attitude that's her real strength. She's pragmatic; she understands the value of compromise. Whereas you...'

He paused, and Nola felt her skin tighten. That was Anna in a nutshell. But how could Ram know that? They'd only met once, when they'd signed the contracts.

And then her muscles tensed, her body squirming with nerves at what he might be about to reveal about her.

'You, on the other hand, are a rebel.'

Reaching out, he ran his hand lightly over her sleeve and she felt a thrill like the jolt of electricity. This wasn't like any conversation she'd ever had. It was more like a dance—a dazzling dance with quick, complicated steps that only they understood.

She swallowed. 'What kind of rebel works *for* the system?'

Beneath the lights, his eyes gleamed like brushed steel. 'You might look corporate on the outside, but if I scratched the surface I'd find a hacker beneath. Unlike your partner—unlike most people, really— you like to cross boundaries, take risks. You're not motivated by money; you like the challenge.'

The hum of chatter and laughter faded around them and a pulse began to beat loudly inside her head. Reaching forward to pick up her glass, she cleared her throat with difficulty.

'You're making me sound a lot edgier than I am,' she said quickly. 'I'm actually just a "white hat".'

'Of course you are!'

Ram shifted in his seat, his thigh brushing against her leg so that her hand twitched around the stem of the glass. It was a gambler's tell— a tiny, visible sign of the tension throbbing between them.

'It's not like I'd ever catch you hanging out in some grimy internet café with a bunch of wannabe anarchists.'

He lounged back in his seat, one eyebrow lifted, challenging her to contradict him.

Remembering their first meeting, Nola felt her heart beat faster, her stomach giving way to that familiar mix of apprehension and fascination, the sense that there was something pulling them inexorably closer.

But even as she felt her skin grow warm his teasing words stirred something inside her. Suddenly the desire to tease him back was overwhelming—to put the heat on *him*, to watch those grey eyes turn molten.

'Actually, wannabe anarchists are usually pretty harmless—like sheep. It's the wolf in sheep's clothing you need to worry about.'

She kept her expression innocent, but heat cascaded down through her belly as his gaze locked onto hers with the intensity of a tractor beam. A small, urgent voice in the back of her head was warning her to back down, to stop playing Russian roulette with the man who'd loaded the gun she was holding to her head.

But then suddenly he smiled, and just like that nothing seemed to matter except being the focus of his undivided attention. It was easy to forget he was self-serving and arrogant…easy to believe that breaking the rules—*her* rules—wouldn't matter just this once.

Her heart began to beat faster.

Except she knew from experience that it *would* matter. And that smile wasn't a challenge. It was a warning—a red light flashing. *Danger! Keep away!*

Breathing in, she gave him a quick, neutral smile of her own. 'Now, this menu!' Holding her smile in place, she forced a casual note into her voice. 'My French is pretty non-existent, so I might need a little help ordering.'

'Don't worry. I speak it fluently.'

'You do?' She gazed at him, torn between disbelief and wonder.

He shrugged. 'My mother always wanted to live in Paris, but it didn't work out. So she sent me to school there.'

Nola frowned. 'Paris! You mean Paris in France?'

'I don't think they speak French in Paris, Texas.'

His face was expressionless. but there was a tension in his shoulders that hadn't been there before.

Her eyes met his, then bounced away. 'That's such a long way from here,' she said slowly.

'I suppose it is.'

Her pulse twitched.

It would have been easy to take his reply at face value, as just another of those glib, offhand remarks people made to keep a conversation running smoothly.

But something had shifted in his voice—or rather left it. The teasing warmth had gone, had been replaced by something cool and dismissive that pricked her skin like the sting of a wasp.

It was her cue to back off—and maybe she would have done so an hour earlier. But this was the first piece of personal information he had ever shared with her.

She cleared her throat. 'So how old were you?'

Along the back of her seat, she could feel the muscles in his arm tensing.

'Seven.' He gazed at her steadily. 'It was a good school. I had a great education there.'

She knew her face had stiffened into some kind of answering smile—she just hoped it looked more convincing than it felt. Nodding, she said quickly, 'I'm sure. And learning another language is such an opportunity.'

'It has its uses.' He spoke tonelessly. 'But I wasn't talking about speaking French. Being away taught me to rely on myself. To trust my own judgement. Great life lessons—and brilliant for business.'

Did he ever think of anything else? Nola wondered. Surely he must have been homesick or lonely? But the expression on his face made it clear that it was definitely time to change the subject.

Glancing down at her menu again, she said quickly, 'So, what do you recommend?'

'That depends on what you like to eat.'

Looking up, she saw with relief that the tightness in his face had eased.

'The fish is great here, and they do fantastic steaks.' He frowned. 'I forgot to ask. You do eat meat?'

She nodded.

'And no allergies?'

His words were innocent enough, but there was a lazy undercurrent in his voice that made the palms of her hands grow damp, and her heart gave a thump as his eyes settled on her face.

'Apart from to me, I mean...'

Her insides tightened, and a prickling heat spread over her cheeks and throat as she gave him a small, tight, polite smile.

'I'm not allergic to you, Mr Walker.' She bit her lip, her eyes meeting his. 'For a start, allergies tend to be involuntary.'

'Oh, I see. So you're *choosing* to ignore this thing between us?'

She swallowed, unable to look away from his dark, mocking gaze.

'If by "ignore" you mean not behave in an unprofessional and inappropriate manner, then, yes, I am,' she said crisply.

He studied her face in silence, and as she gazed into his flawless features a tingling heat seeped through her limbs, cocooning her body so she felt drowsy and blurred around the edges.

'So you do admit that there is something between us?'

His words sent a pulse up her spine, bringing her to her senses instantly, and she felt a rush of adrenaline. Damn him! She was in security. It was her job to keep out unwanted intruders, to keep important data secret. So why was it that she fell into each and every one of his traps with such humiliating ease?

She wasn't even sure how he did it. No one else had ever managed to get under her skin so easily. But he seemed not only able to read her mind, but to turn her inside out so that she had nowhere to hide. It made her feel raw, flayed, vulnerable.

Remembering the last time she had felt so vulnerable, she shivered. Connor's betrayal still had the power to hurt. But, even though she knew now that it was her ego not her heart that he'd damaged, no good was going to come of confessing any of that to Ram—a man who had zero interest in emotions, his own and other people's.

And that was why this conversation was going to stop.

Lifting her chin, she met his gaze with what she hoped was an expression of cool composure.

'I don't think a business meeting is really the right time to have this particular conversation,' she said coolly. 'But, as you have a girlfriend, I'm not sure when or where *would* be right.'

'Girlfriend?' He seemed genuinely surprised. 'If you mean Clio, then, yes, she's female. But "girlfriend"? That would be stretching it. And don't look so outraged. She knows exactly what's on offer, and she's grateful to take it.'

She stared at him in disbelief. 'Grateful! For what? For being fortunate enough to have sex with the great Ramsay Walker?'

'In a nutshell.'

He seemed amused rather than annoyed.

'You surprise me, Ms Mason. Given the nature of your job, I thought you of all people would know that it pays to look beneath the surface.' His eyes gleamed. 'You really shouldn't believe everything you read on the internet.'

A quivering irritation flickered through her brain, like static on the radio.

'Is that right? So, for example, all those times you're meant to have said you don't want to get married or have children—that was all lies? You were misquoted?'

Ram stared past her, felt the breath whipping out of him. Used to women who sought to soothe and seduce, he felt her directness like a rogue wave, punching him off his feet. Who did she think she was, to question him like this? To put him, his life, under a spotlight?

But beneath his exasperation he could feel his body responding to the heat sparking in her eyes.

Ignoring his uneven heartbeat, he met her furious blue gaze. 'I'm not in the business of explaining myself, Ms Mason. But this one time I'll answer your question. I wasn't misquoted. Everything I said was and is true. I have no desire whatsoever to marry or have children.'

That was an understatement. Marriage had never been a priority for him. Parenthood even less so. And for good reason. Both might appear to offer security and satisfaction, but it had been a long time since he'd believed in the myths they promised.

Out in the bay, the Opera House was lit up, its sails gleaming ghost-white. But it was the darkness that drew his gaze. For a moment he let it blot out the twisting mass of feelings that were rising up inside him, unbidden and unwelcome.

Commitment came at a cost, and he knew that the debt would never be paid. A wife and a child were a burden—a responsibility he simply didn't want. Had never once wanted.

And he didn't intend to start now.

Leaning back in his chair, he shrugged. 'Marriage and parenthood are just a Mobius strip of emotional scenes that quite frankly I can do without. I'm sorry if that offends your romantic sensibilities, Ms Mason, but that's how I choose to live my life.'

There was a moment of absolute silence.

Nola drew a breath. By 'romantic', he clearly meant deluded, soppy and hopelessly outdated. It was also obvious that he thought her resistance to him was driven not by logic but by a desire for something more meaningful than passion.

She felt a pulse of anger beneath her skin. Maybe it was time to disabuse him of that belief.

Eyes narrowing, she stared at him coldly. 'Sorry to disillusion you, Mr Walker, but I don't have any "romantic sensibilities". I don't crave a white wedding. Nor am I hunting for a husband to make my life complete. So if I actually had an opinion on how you live your life it would be that I have no problem with it at all.'

His watched—no—*inspected* her in silence, so that the air seemed to swell painfully in her lungs.

'But you do have a problem…' He paused, and the intent expression on his face made her insides tighten and her throat grow dry and scratchy. 'You think I say something different in private to the women you refer to as my "girlfriends".'

He shook his head slowly. 'Then it's my turn to disillusion you. I don't make false promises. Why would I? It's not as if I need to. I always get exactly what I want in the end.'

She shook her head. 'You're so arrogant.'

'I'm being honest. Isn't that what you wanted from me?'

'I don't want anything from you,' she said hoarsely, trying to ignore the heat scalding her skin, 'except a salary and a reference. I certainly have no interest in being some accessory to your louche lifestyle.'

Watching his mouth curl into a slow, sexy smile, she felt her stomach drop as though the legs of her chair had snapped.

'So why are you blushing?' he asked softly. 'Surely not because of my "louche lifestyle". I thought you were more open-minded than that.'

She glowered at him.

'I'm as open-minded as the next woman. But not if it means being a part of your harem. That's never been one of my fantasies.'

'Sadly, I'm going to have to put your fantasies on hold,' he said softly, raising his hand in a gesture of greeting to the two tall blond men who were weaving their way towards them. 'Our guests are here. But maybe we could discuss them after dinner?'

* * *

'I think that's the first time I've seen you relax since you arrived.'

Glancing up at Ram, Nola frowned.

Dinner was over, and his limo had dropped them back at the RWI building. Now they were standing in the lift.

Like many of his remarks, it could be read in so many ways. But she was too tired to do anything but take it at face value.

'It was fun,' she said simply. 'I enjoyed the food and the company.'

He did a mock stagger. 'I'm flattered.'

Glancing up, she saw that he was smiling, and she felt a panicky rush of nerves. In daylight, Ram Walker was flawless but unattainable. Now it was night-time, and beneath the low lighting, with his top button undone and a shadow of stubble grazing his face, he looked like the perfect after-dark female fantasy.

But the point about fantasies was that they were never supposed to become reality, she told herself quickly.

Shaking her head, she gave him a small, careful smile. 'I suppose it hasn't occurred to you that I might be talking about Craig and Will?'

His eyes gleamed. 'Nope.'

She swallowed. 'They're nice people.'

'And I'm not?'

Her throat felt as though it was closing up. And, was it her imagination, or was the lift getting smaller and hotter?

'You can be,' she said cautiously. She felt her pulse twitch beneath his gaze. 'But I don't know you very well. We don't know each other very well.'

Suddenly she was struggling to breathe, and her heart was beating very fast.

He smiled. 'Oh, I think we know each other very well, Nola!'

Her stomach dropped as though the lift cable had suddenly snapped, and somewhere at the edge of her vision stars were flickering—only that couldn't be right for they weren't outside.

'And I think you're a lot like me,' he said softly. 'You're focused, and determined, and you like breaking the rules. Even when you're scared of the consequences.'

There was a tiny shift in the air...softer than a sigh.

She watched, dry-mouthed, her stomach twisting into knots as he reached out and ran his finger along her cheekbone. She could feel her heartbeat echoing inside her head like footsteps fleeing. As she should be.

Except that she couldn't move—could hardly breathe.

He moved closer, sliding his hand through her hair.

'When I met you in that café you took my breath away. You still do.'

There was silence as she struggled to speak, struggled against the ridiculous pleasure his words provoked. Pleasure she knew she shouldn't acknowledge, let alone feel. Not for her boss anyway.

But maybe she was making too big a deal about that. He might be a CEO, but he was just a man, and as a woman she was his equal. Besides, as of tomorrow he wouldn't even be her boss.

The thought jumped inside her head like popping candy, and then somehow her hand was on his arm, the magnetic pull between them impossible to resist.

'Ram…' She whispered his name and he stared down at her mutely. His eyes were dark and fierce, and she could see that he was struggling for control.

She felt a shiver of panic tumble down her spine. But why?

What did she care if he was struggling? So was she. Like her, he was fighting himself—fighting this desire.

Desire.

The word jangled inside her head like a warning bell, for was desire a big enough reason to play truth or dare with this man? After all, she knew the risks, knew the consequences.

Her head was spinning. Memories of that first kiss with Connor were slip-sliding into an image of his face, resentful and distant, on that last day.

But there was no reason it would be the same with Ram.

Nola knew she had been reckless with Connor—clueless, really. She'd jumped off the highest board and hoped for what? Love? A soulmate? A future? But *this* was never going to be anything but lust. There was no expectation. No need to make promises.

And, most importantly, there would be no consequences. After tomorrow they would never see one another again. It would be a perfect moment of pure passion. So why shouldn't she give in to it?

But even as the question formed in her mind she knew two things. One, it was purely rhetorical. And two, it was too late.

The warmth of his body had melted away the last of her resistance; the battle was already lost.

And, as though he could read her mind, Ram leaned forward and kissed her.

Groaning softly, he reached out blindly for the wall of the lift, trying to steady himself. He'd expected to feel something—hell, how could he not after the tension that had been building between them for weeks?—but the touch of her lips on his was like being knocked sideways by a rogue wave.

His head was spinning. Somewhere, the world was still turning, but it didn't matter. All that mattered was here and now and Nola. Her body was melting into him, moving as he moved, her breath and his breath were one and the same. He felt her lips part and, deepening the kiss, he pulled her closer.

As the doors opened he pulled her against him and out of the lift. Hands sliding over each other, they staggered backwards, drunkenly banging into walls, barely noticing the impact. Somehow they reached his office, and as he pushed open the door they stumbled into the room as one.

Nola reached out for him, her fingers clutching the front of his shirt. He could feel her heart pounding, hear her breath coming in gasps. She pulled him closer and, groaning softly, he wrapped his fingers around hers and dragged her arms behind her back, holding her captive.

Ram shuddered. His heart was pounding so hard he thought it might burst and, reaching down, he jerked her closer, crushing her body against his. But it wasn't enough. He wanted more. Breathing out shakily, he nudged her backwards, guiding her towards the sofa.

As they slid onto the cushions he dragged his mouth from hers and she gazed up at him, her eyes huge and dazed.

His breath caught in his throat. He wanted her

so badly, but he needed to know that she wanted what *he* wanted—what he could give.

'I don't do for ever. Or happy-ever-after. This is about now. About you and me. If you're hoping for something more than that—'

In answer, she looped her arm about his neck, gripping him tightly. 'Stop talking and kiss me,' she whispered, her fingers tugging at his arms, his shirt, his belt.

He knew that relief must be showing on his face, but for once he didn't care that he'd shown his true feelings. She had said what he wanted to hear and, lowering his mouth, he kissed her fiercely. As her lips parted he caught hold of the front of her blouse and tugged it loose.

Instantly he felt his groin harden. For a moment his eyes fed hungrily on the soft, pale curve of her stomach, and the small rounded breasts in the black lace bra.

She was beautiful—every bit as beautiful as he'd imagined.

And he couldn't wait a moment longer.

Leaning forward, he fumbled with the fastening of her bra and it was gone. Then he lowered his mouth to her bare breast, feeling the nipple harden beneath his tongue.

Nola whimpered. His tongue was pulling her upwards. She felt as if she was floating; her blood was lighter than air.

Helplessly, she let her head fall back, arching her spine so that her hips were pressing against his thighs. Her head was spinning, her body so hot and tight with need that she hardly knew who she was. All she knew was that she wanted him— wanted to feel him on her and in her.

She couldn't fight it anymore—couldn't fight herself.

Desperately she squirmed beneath him, freeing him with her fingers. She heard him groan, then a choking sound deep in his throat as she slid her hand around his erection.

For a moment he steadied himself above her, the muscles of his arms straining to hold his weight, his beautiful clean profile tensing with the effort.

Breathing out unsteadily, he gazed down at her. 'What about—?' he began. 'Are you protected?'

Nola gazed at him feverishly. She didn't want to talk. Didn't want anything to come between them—and, besides, there was no need.

'It's fine,' she whispered.

His eyes flared, his expression shifting, his face growing tauter as slowly he pushed the hem of her skirt up around her hips. She shivered, the sudden rush of air cooling her overheated skin, and then she breathed in sharply as he pressed the palm of his hand against the liquid ache between her thighs.

Helplessly, eagerly, she pressed back, and then

suddenly he pulled her mouth up to meet his and pushed into her.

His fingers were bumping over her ribcage, his touch making her heartbeat stagger. She reached up, sliding her hand through his hair, scraping his scalp. The ache inside her was beating harder and faster and louder, the urge to pull him closer and deeper overwhelming her so that suddenly she was moving desperately, reaching for him, pressing against him.

She felt a sting of ecstasy—a white heat spreading out like a supernova—and then she arched against him, her breath shuddering in her throat. As her muscles spasmed around him he groaned her name and tensed, filling her completely.

CHAPTER THREE

NOLA WOKE WITH a start.

For a moment she lay in the darkness, her brain still only on pilot light, wondering what had woken her. Almost immediately the warmth of her bed began tugging her back towards sleep and, stifling a yawn, she wriggled drowsily against the source of the heat.

And froze.

Not just her body, but her blood, her heartbeat. Even the breath in her throat hardened like ice, so that suddenly she was rigid—like a tightrope walker who'd just looked down beyond the rope.

Head spinning, she slid her hand tentatively over her thigh and touched the solid, sleeping form of Ram. As her fingers brushed against him she felt him stir and shift closer, his arm curving over her waist, and instantly she was completely, fiercely awake.

Around her the air stilled and the darkness closed in on her. Someone—Ram?—had turned off the lights in the office. Or maybe they just switched off automatically. But her eyes were adjusting now, and she could just make out the solid bulk of his desk. And strewn across the floor, distorted into strange, unfamiliar shapes, were their discarded clothes.

Picturing how they had torn them off in their hurry to feel each other's naked skin, she felt her cheeks grow hot and she blew out a breath.

Finally they'd done it. They'd had sex.

Her skin tightened in the darkness, her heartbeat fluttering, as a smile pulled at her mouth.

Sex! That made it sound so ordinary, or mechanical. But it had been anything but that.

Beside her, Ram shifted in his sleep, and the damp warmth of his body sent a tremor of hot, panicky excitement over her skin.

Remembering his fierce, hard mouth on hers, his hands roaming at will over her aching, desperate body, she pressed her hand against her lips, her stomach flip-flopping as she felt the slight puffiness where he'd kissed her again and again.

She'd expected the sex to be incredible. But now, with his hard, muscular arm curled possessively around her waist, and her body still throbbing from the frenzied release of their lovemaking, she knew that what she and Ram had shared had been more than incredible.

It had been—she searched for a word—it had been *transformative*. Beautiful and wild and breathless, flaring up like a forest fire, so hot and fast that it had consumed everything in its path straight to the sea.

And then afterwards calm, a peace such as she had never known. Just the two of them glowing in each other's arms, spent, sated, their bodies seeping into one another.

It had felt so right. *He'd* felt so right.

She shivered again. Ram had been the lover she'd imagined but never expected to meet in real life. Intuitive, generous, his touch had been a masterclass in power and precision.

He had demanded more from her than she had been willing to give, but she had yielded, for it had been impossible to resist the strength of her desire. The intensity of his.

Over and over he had pulled her against him, touching her, finding the place where liquid heat gathered, using his lips, his hands, his body to stir and torment her until the blood had beaten inside her so hard and so fast she'd thought she would pass out. She had been frantic and feverish—hadn't known who or where she was. Her entire being—every thought, every beat of her heart—had been concentrated on him, on his mouth, his body, his fingertips…

A memory of exactly what he'd done with those fingers dropped into her head and she squirmed, pressing her thighs together.

She couldn't understand why she was feeling this way. Why she had responded so strongly to a man she barely knew and didn't even really like.

She'd loved Connor—or at least she'd thought she had—yet sex with him had only ever been satisfying. Whereas with Ram it had been sublime.

It made no sense.

But then, nothing she'd thought, said or done in the last twenty-four hours had even come close to making sense. Not least sleeping with the man who, for the next twelve hours or so, was still her boss.

Her breath felt thick and scratchy in her throat.

Oh, she knew why she'd done it.

Ram Walker was not your average man. Even just being in his orbit made her feel as if someone had handed her the keys to a top-spec sports car and told her to put her foot down. He was exhilarating, irresistible.

But she knew from sleeping with Connor that giving in to temptation had consequences. Messy, unexpected and painful consequences. And so she'd waited until now, until the day before her contract ended, to give in, believing that she was being smart.

Believing it would just be one perfect night of pure pleasure.

Her skin grew hot, then cold.

She'd thought it would be so easy. Not just the sex, but the aftermath. Maybe there might be a few awkward moments. But surely nothing too dramatic or life-changing. After all, she barely knew Ram.

It had never once crossed her mind that she would feel this way—so moved, so alive.

She'd thought once would be enough. That her body would be satisfied and she could forget him and move on.

She almost laughed out loud.

Forget him!

As if she could ever forget him.

Right now, there was only him.

It was as though he'd wiped her mind—erased every memory and experience she'd ever had. And it wasn't only the past he'd obliterated. Her future would never be the same now either. How could it be after last night? She might not have a crystal ball, but she didn't need one to know that sex was never going to be as good with any other man.

But what if today was the last time she ever saw Ram?

Was she really that naive? So stupid as to imagine they were done? That she could put last night in a box, wrap it up neatly with a bow and that would be it.

Her pulse began to race.

Since breaking up with Connor she'd been so careful. She'd had a couple of short relationships, but at the first hint of anything serious she had broken them off. It had seemed safer, given her bad luck when it came to men. Or was it bad judgement?

Her father, Richard, had been charming—financially generous. But even before her parents' divorce he had been unreliable—often disappearing without explanation, and always utterly incapable of remembering anything to do with his wife and daughter, from birthdays to parents' evenings.

Then she'd met Connor—sweet, funny Connor—who had cared about everything from saving the planet to the trainers he wore. Miraculously, he had cared about her too, so she'd thought it would be different with him.

And it had been—for a time.

Until he'd betrayed her trust...shared the most private details of their life together over a pint in the pub. And then not even stepped up to defend her reputation.

She almost laughed, but felt more as if she was about to cry.

Her reputation.

It made her sound like some foolish eighteenth-century heroine who'd let the wrong man pick up her fan. But that was what she'd felt like. Foolish and powerless. And the fact that her supposed boyfriend had sacrificed her to impress his mates still had the power to make her curl up inside with misery.

Breathing out silently, she closed her eyes.

She'd vowed never again to trust her judgement. And with Ram she hadn't needed to. Her opinion of him was irrelevant; the facts spoke for themselves.

Even before they'd met in that café in Sydney she'd known his reputation as a ruthless womaniser. Yet she'd still gone ahead and slept with him.

And why?

Because she'd become complacent.

She'd assumed, like last time, that the worst-case scenario would be the two of them having to work in the same building. Now, though, she could see that geography didn't matter, and that the worst-case scenario was happening inside her head. And it was all to do with *him*, and how he'd made her feel.

But she couldn't think about this anymore. Not with his body so warm and solid beside her.

Her breathing faltered.

It was time to leave.

Moving carefully, so as not to wake him, she slid out from beneath his arm and began groping in the darkness for her discarded bra and shoes. Her bag was harder to find, but finally she located it by one of the armchairs.

Clutching her blouse in one hand, she tiptoed to the door and gently pushed down the handle. There was a tiny but unmistakable click and she held her breath. But there was no sound from within the darkened office and slowly, carefully, she pulled open the door and slid through it into the empty corridor.

As she waited for the lift her heartbeat sounded like raindrops on a tin roof. Every second felt like a day, and she couldn't shift the feeling that at any moment she would hear Ram's voice or his footsteps in the darkness.

Pressing her forehead against the wall, she breathed out slowly. She should be feeling relief, and in some ways she was, for now she wouldn't have to go through that horrific about-last-night conversation, or the alternative—the awkward let's-pretend-it-never-happened version.

But she couldn't help feeling that somehow she was making a mistake. That what had happened between them had been so rare, so right, that she shouldn't just walk away from it.

She turned and gazed hesitantly down the darkened corridor.

Was she doing the right thing?

Or was she about to do something she'd regret?

But what would happen if she stayed?

Her heart was racing like a steeplechaser. What should she do?

She needed help. Fifty/fifty? Ask the audience?

She felt a rush of relief.

Phone a friend.

Stepping into the lift, she pulled out her mobile. It was four in the morning here, which made it two in the afternoon in Barbados. She would let it ring three times and then hang up.

Anna picked up on the second ring.

'Hi, you. This is a surprise…'

She paused, and for a moment Nola could almost picture her friend's face, the slight furrow between her eyes as she mentally calculated the time difference between the Caribbean and Australia.

'Have you been pulling an all-nighter or did you just randomly get up to watch the sunrise?'

Anna's voice was as calm as ever, but there was a brightness to it that Nola recognised as concern. And, despite everything, that made her feel calmer.

She swallowed. 'Neither. Look, I'm not hurt or anything, but…' She breathed out slowly. 'I've just done something really stupid. At least I think it was really stupid.'

There was the shortest of silences, and then Anna said firmly, 'In that case I'll get Robbie to make me a Rum Punch and you can tell me all about it.'

It was not the daylight creeping into his office that woke Ram. Nor was it the faint but aggravating hum of some kind of machinery. It was Nola.

Or rather the fact—the quite incredible fact—that at some unspecified point in the night she had gone.

Left.

Done a runner.

Hightailed it.

He felt a sudden sharp, inexplicable spasm of… of what? Irritation? Outrage? Disappointment?

No. A twitch ran down his spine and, breathing out, he sat up slowly and ran his hand over the stubble already shadowing his jaw. It was shock. That was all.

Sitting up, he stared in disbelief around the empty office.

This had *never* happened. Ever. And, despite the evidence proving that it had, he still couldn't quite believe his eyes.

His heart started to beat faster. But, really, should he be that surprised? Every single time he thought he'd got Nola Mason all figured out she threw him a curveball that not only knocked him off his feet but left him wondering who she really was.

Who *he* really was.

He scowled. In this instance that should have been an easy question to answer.

He was the one who dressed and left.

He was always the one who chose the venue, and he never slept over.

Spending the night with a woman hinted too

strongly at a kind of commitment he'd spent a lifetime choosing to avoid.

His face hardened. That didn't mean, though, that women upped and left him.

But, squinting into the pale grey light that was seeping into the room, he was forced to accept that on this occasion, with this woman, it did mean exactly that.

Which should be a good thing. Most women were tedious about their need to be held, or to talk, or to plan the next date, even when he couldn't have made it any clearer that none of the above was on offer.

Only for some reason Nola's departure felt premature.

Incomprehensible.

Maybe he was just overthinking it.

But why did her leaving seem to matter so much?

Probably because, although superficially she might have seemed different, he'd assumed in the end that she would behave like every other woman he knew. Only nothing about last night had turned out as he'd imagined it would.

He'd thought he was seducing her, but he'd never lost control like that.

He certainly hadn't planned to have sex with her *here*, on the sofa in his office. But could he really be blamed for what had happened?

The tension between had been building from the moment they'd first met. In the restaurant it had been so intense, so powerful, he was surprised the other diners hadn't been sucked in by its gravitational pull.

She'd been as shaken by it as him—he was sure of it—and in the lift she had responded to his kiss so fiercely, and with such lack of inhibition, that he'd never got as far as inviting her back to his apartment.

Remembering that beat before they'd kissed, he felt his heart trip, heat and hunger tangling inside him. Watching that to-hell-with-you expression on her face grow fiercer, then soften as she melted into him, he'd wanted her so badly that he would have taken there and then in the lift if the doors hadn't opened.

Glancing round his office, his eyes homed in on his discarded shirt and he felt suddenly breathless, winded by the memory of how he'd sped her through the building with no real awareness of what he was doing, no conscious thought at all, just a need to have her in the most primitive way possible.

Reaching down, he picked his shirt up from the floor and slid his arms carelessly into the sleeves.

He hadn't hurt her. He would never do that. But he hadn't recognised himself. Hadn't recognised that fire, that urgency, that need—

The word snagged inside his head. No, not *need*.

It had been a long time since he had let himself *need* anyone. Not since he'd been a child, fighting misery and loneliness in a school on the other side of the world from his mother. Needing people, being needed, was something he'd avoided all his adult life, and whatever he might have felt for Nola he knew it couldn't have been that.

No, what he'd felt for Nola had been lust. And, like hunger and thirst, once it had been satisfied it would be forgotten. *She* would be forgotten.

And that was what mattered. After months of feeling distracted and on edge, he could finally get back to focusing on his work.

After all, that was the real reason he'd wanted to sleep with her. To soothe the burn of frustration that had not only tested his self-control but made it impossible for him to focus on the biggest product launch of his career.

Now, though, just as he had with every other female he'd bedded, he could draw a line under her and get on with the rest of his life.

Straightening his cuffs, he stood up and walked briskly towards the door.

Ten hours later he was wrapping up the last meeting of the day.

'Right, if there's nothing else then I think we'll finish up here.'

It was five o'clock.

Ram glanced casually around the boardroom, saw his heads of department were already collecting their laptops and paperwork. His loathing of meetings was legendary among his staff, as was his near fanatical insistence that they start *and* end on time.

Pulling his laptop in front of him, he flipped it open as they began to leave the room.

The day had passed with grinding slowness.

Nothing had seemed to hold his attention, or maybe he simply hadn't been able to concentrate. But, either way, his thoughts had kept drifting off from whatever spreadsheet or proposal he was supposed to be discussing, and his head had filled with memories of the night before.

More specifically, memories of Nola—her body straddling his, her face softening as his own body grew harder than it had ever been...

He gritted his teeth. For some reason she had got under his skin in a way no woman ever had before. He'd even fallen asleep holding her in his arms. But for once intimacy had felt natural, right.

Staring down blankly at his computer screen, he felt his chest tighten. So what if it had felt right? He'd held her *in his sleep.* He hadn't even been conscious. And of course he would like to have sex with Nola again. He was a normal heterosexual man, and she was a beautiful, sexy woman.

Abruptly his muscles tensed, his eyes narrowing infinitesimally as through the open door he caught a glimpse of gleaming dark hair.

Nola! His stomach tightened involuntarily and he felt a rush of anticipation.

All day he'd been expecting to bump into her, had half imagined that she might seek him out. But now he realised that wouldn't be her way. She'd want it to play out naturally—like the tide coming in and going out again.

He breathed out sharply, his pulse zigzagging through his veins like a thread pulled through fabric, and before he even knew what he was doing he had crossed the room and yanked open the door.

But the corridor was empty.

Anger stuttered across his skin.

What the—? Why hadn't she come in to talk to him? She *must* have seen him.

Breathing out slowly, he stalked swiftly through the corridor to his office.

Jenny, his secretary, glanced up from her computer, her eyes widening at the expression on his face.

'Get Nola Mason on the phone. Tell her I want her in my office in the next five minutes.'

Slamming his office door, he strode across the room and stared furiously out of the window.

Was this some kind of a game?

Hopefully not—for *her* sake.

There was a knock at the door, and he felt a rush of satisfaction at having dragged Nola away from whatever it was she'd been doing.

'Come in,' he said curtly.

'Mr Walker—'

He turned, his face hardening as he saw Jenny, hovering in the doorway.

She smiled nervously. 'I'm sorry, Mr Walker. I was just going to tell you, but you went into your office before—'

He frowned impatiently. 'Tell me what?'

'Ms Mason can't come right now.'

'Can't or won't?' he snapped.

Jenny blinked. 'Oh, I'm sure she would if she were here, Mr Walker. But she's not here. She left about an hour ago. For the airport.'

Ram stared at her in silence, his eyes narrowing.

The airport?

'I—I thought you knew,' she stammered.

'I did.' He gave her a quick, curt smile. 'It must have slipped my mind. Thank you, Jenny.'

As the door closed his phone buzzed in his jacket and he reached for it, glancing distractedly down at the screen. And then his heart began to beat rhythmically in his chest.

It was an email.

From *Nola_Mason@CyberAngels.org*.

The corner of his mouth twisted, and then the

words on the screen seemed to slip sideways as he slowly read, then reread, the email.

Dear Mr Walker

I am writing to confirm that in accordance with our agreement, today will be the last day of my employment at RWI. My colleague, Anna Harris—nee Mackenzie—and I will, of course, be in close contact with the on-site team, and remain available for any questions you may have.

I look forward to the successful completion of the project, and I wish to take this opportunity to thank you for all your personal input.

Nola Mason

Ram stared blankly at the email.

Was this some kind of a joke?

Slowly, his heart banging against his ribs like bailiffs demanding overdue rent, he reread it.

No, it wasn't a joke. It was a brush-off.

He read it again, his anger mounting with every word. Oh, it was all very polite, but there could be no mistaking the thank-you-but-I'm-done undertone. Why else would she have included that choice little remark at the bottom?

I wish to take this opportunity to thank you for all your personal input.

His fingers tightened around the phone.

Personal input!

He could barely see the screen through the veil of anger in front of his eyes, and it didn't help that he knew he was behaving irrationally—hypocritically, even. For in the past he'd ended liaisons with far less charm and courtesy.

But this was the woman he was paying to protect his business from unwanted intruders. Why, then, had he let her get past the carefully constructed emotional defences he'd built between himself and the world?

CHAPTER FOUR

Three months later

GLANCING UP AT the chalkboard above her head, Nola sighed. It was half past ten and the coffee shop was filling up, and as usual there was just too much choice. Today though, she had a rare morning off, and she wasn't about to waste the whole of it choosing a hot drink! Not even in Seattle, the coffee-drinking capital of the world.

Stepping forward, she smiled apologetically at the barista behind the counter. 'Just a green tea. Drink in. Oh, and one of those Danish, please. The cinnamon sort. Thanks.'

The sun was shining, but it was still not quite warm enough to sit outside, so she made her way to a table with a view of Elliott Bay.

Shrugging off her jacket, she leaned back in her seat, enjoying the sensation of sunlight on her face. Most of her time at work was spent alone in an office, hunched over a screen, so whenever she had any free time she liked to spend it outside. And her favourite place was right here, on the waterfront.

It was a little bit touristy. But then she *was* a tourist. And, besides, even if it did cater mainly to visitors, the restaurants still served amazingly fresh seafood and the coffee shops were a great place to relax and people-watch.

It was two weeks since she'd arrived in Seattle. And three months since she'd left Sydney. Three months of picking over the bones of her impulsive behaviour. Of wondering why she had ever thought that the consequences of sleeping with her boss would be less messy than sleeping with any other colleague?

Her pulse hopscotched forward. It was a little late to start worrying about consequences now. Particularly when one of them was a baby.

Breathing out slowly, she glanced down at her stomach and ran her hand lightly over the small rounded bump.

She had never imagined having a child. Her parents' unhappy marriage and eventual divorce had not exactly encouraged her to think of matrimony as the fairy-tale option that many of her friends, including Anna, believed it to be.

Being a mother, like being married, had always been something she thought happened to other people. Had she thought about it at all, she would probably have wanted the father of her baby to be a gentle, easy-going, thoughtful man.

She took another sip of tea.

So not Ram Walker, then.

And yet here she was, carrying his baby.

Across the café a young couple sat drinking *lattes*, gazing dotingly at a baby in a buggy. They looked like a photoshoot for the perfect modern family, and suddenly the cup in her hand felt heavy. Almost as heavy as her heart. For it was a life her child would never enjoy.

Not least because she hadn't told Ram about the baby.

And nor would she.

Had he shown any sign, any hint that he wanted to be a father, she would have told him the moment she'd found out. But some men just weren't cut out for relationships and commitment, and Ram was one of them.

He'd said so to her face, so it had been easy at first to feel that her silence was justified—especially when she was still struggling not just with the shock of finding out she was pregnant but with nausea and an exhaustion that made getting dressed feel like a tough mission.

Only now, when finally she was in a fit enough state to think, she was almost as overwhelmed with guilt as she had been with nausea.

Evening after evening had been spent silently arguing with herself over whether or not she should tell him about the baby. But with each passing day she'd convinced herself that there really was no point in letting him know.

He'd clearly stated that he didn't want to be a

father, and she knew from the way he lived his life that he wasn't capable of being one.

She didn't mean biologically. He clearly could father a child—and had. But what kind of a father would he be? His relationships with women lasted days, not years—not much use for raising a child to adulthood. Their brief affair had given her first-hand experience of his limited attention span. That night in his office she had felt as though he was floating through her veins. But afterwards he'd barely acknowledged the email she'd sent him. Just sent a single sentence thanking her for her services.

Her face felt hot. Was that the real reason why she hadn't told him about the baby? Her pride? Her ego? A yearning to keep her memories of that night intact and not made ugly by the truth? The truth that he'd never wanted anything more than a one-night stand. Never wanted her *or* this baby.

She felt the hot sting of tears behind her eyes as silently she questioned her motives again. But, no, it wasn't pride or sentimentality that was stopping her from saying anything.

It was him. It was Ram.

She didn't need to confront him to know that he wouldn't want to know about the baby, or be a father, or be in their lives. Whatever connection there had been between them had ended when she'd crept out of his office in the early hours of that morning. Nothing would change that, so why put herself through the misery of having him spell it out in black and white?

She shifted in her seat. So now she was three months pregnant, unmarried, living out of a suitcase—and happy.

It was true that she sometimes got a little freaked out at the thought of being solely responsible for the baby growing inside her. But she knew she could bring a child up on her own—better than if Ram was involved.

Her mum had done it and, besides, Anna and Robbie would be there for her—when she finally got round to telling them.

She felt a twinge of guilt.

Unlike with Ram, she didn't have any doubts about telling her friends about the baby. Quite the opposite. She wanted them to know. But by the time she'd done a test she'd been in Seattle, struggling with morning sickness. Besides, she wanted to tell her friend face-to-face, not over the—

Her phone rang and, glancing down at the screen, she frowned. It was Anna. Quickly, she answered it.

'That is so weird. I was literally just thinking about you.'

Anna snorted. 'Really? What happened? Did you eat some shortbread and finally remember your old pal in Scotland?'

'I spoke to you three days ago,' Nola protested.

'And you said you'd call back. But what happens? Nothing. No text. No email…'

'I've been busy.'

'Doing what?' Anna paused. 'No, let me guess. Drinking coffee?'

Nola smiled. Since her arrival in Seattle, it was a private joke between them that Nola was drinking coffee every time her friend called.

Tucking the phone under her chin, she smiled. 'Actually, it's green tea, and it's delicious. And the Danish isn't bad either!'

'You're eating a Danish? That's fantastic.'

The relief in Anna's voice caught Nola off guard. They might barely have seen one another over the last few months but she knew her friend had been worried about her, and if she wasn't going to tell her about the baby, the least she could do was put Anna's mind at rest.

'Yeah, you heard it here first. The appetite's back. Pizzerias across the entire state of Washington are rejoicing! In fact I might even get a national holiday named after me.'

Anna laughed. 'I always said you had Italian roots.'

'Was it my blue eyes or my pale skin that gave it away?' Nola said teasingly. 'Okay, that's enough of your amateur psychology, Dr Harris. Tell me why you've rung.'

There was a slight pause.

'You mean I need something more than just being bossy?'

Nola frowned. There was something odd about her friend's voice. She sounded nervous, hesitant. 'I don't know—do you?'

There was a short silence, then Anna sighed. 'Yes. I still can't believe it happened, but…you know how clumsy I am? Well, I was out walking yesterday with Robbie, and I tripped. Guess what? I broke my foot.'

Relief, smooth and warm, surged over Nola's skin.

'Oh, thank goodness.' She frowned. 'I don't mean thank goodness you broke your foot—I just thought it was going to be something worse.' She breathed out. 'Are you okay? Does it hurt? Have you got one of those crazy boot things?'

'I'm fine. It doesn't hurt anymore and, yeah, I've got a boot. But, Noles…'

Anna paused and Nola felt the air grow still around her.

'But, Noles, what?' she said slowly.

'I can't fly for another week. It's something to do with broken bones making you more at risk of blood clots, so—'

Nola felt her ribcage contract. Glancing down, she noticed that her hands were shaking. But she'd read the email. She knew what was coming.

'So you want me to go to Sydney?'

Nola swallowed. Even just saying the words out loud made panic grip her around the throat.

'I really didn't want to ask you, and ordinarily I'd just postpone it. But the launch is so close.' There was another infinitesimal pause. 'And we *are* under contract.'

Anna sounded so wretched that Nola was instantly furious with herself.

Of course she would go to Sydney. Her friend had been a shoulder to cry on after she'd slept with Ram and generally fallen apart. She damn well wasn't going to make her sweat and feel guilty for asking one tiny favour.

'I know, and I understand—it's fine,' she heard herself say.

'Are you sure? I thought there might be a problem—'

There definitely *would* be a problem, Nola thought dully. About six feet of problem, with tousled dark hair and cheekbones that could sharpen steel. But it would be *her* problem, not Anna's.

'There won't be!' Nola shook her head, trying to shake off the leaden feeling in her chest. 'And it's me who should be sorry. Moping around and making a huge fuss about some one-night stand.'

'You didn't make a fuss,' Anna said indignantly, sounding more like herself. 'You made a mistake. And if he wasn't paying us such a huge sum of money, I'd tell him where he could stick his global launch.'

Nola laughed. 'Let's wait until the money clears and then we can tell him together. Look, please don't worry, Anna. It'll be fine. It's not as if he's going to be making an effort to see me.'

'Oh, you don't need to worry about that,' Anna said quickly. 'I checked before I called you. He's in New York on some business trip. He won't be back for at least five days, so you definitely won't have to see him. Not that you'd have much to say to him even if he was there.'

Hanging up, Nola curled her arms around her waist protectively.

Except that she did.

She had a lot to say.

Only she had no intention of saying any of it to Ram—ever.

Glancing out of the window of his limo, Ram stared moodily up at the RWI building with none of the usual excitement and pride he felt at seeing the headquarters of his company. His trip to New York had been productive and busy—there had been the usual hectic round of meetings—but for the first time ever he had wanted to come home early.

As the car slowed he frowned. He still didn't understand why he'd decided to shorten his trip.

But then, right now he didn't understand a lot of what was happening in his life, for it seemed to be changing in ways he couldn't control or predict.

Nodding at the receptionists on the front desk, he strode through the foyer and took the lift up to the twenty-second floor. Closing the door to his office, he stared disconsolately out of the window.

The launch date was rapidly approaching, but he was struggling to find any enthusiasm and energy for what amounted to the biggest day of his business career.

Nor was he even faintly excited about any of the beautiful, sexy women who were pursuing him with the determination and dedication of hungry cheetahs hunting an impala.

Why did he feel like this? And why was he feeling like it *now*?

He gritted his teeth. He knew the answer to both those questions. In fact it was the same answer. For, despite his having tried to erase her from his mind, *Nola* was the answer, the punchline, the coda to every single question and thought he'd had since she'd left Australia.

It might have been okay if it was just every now and then, but the reality was that Nola was never far from his thoughts. Even though she'd been gone for months now, every time he saw a mass of long dark hair he was still sure it was her. And each time that it wasn't he felt the same excitement, and disappointment, then fury.

There was a knock at the door, and when he was sure his face would give away nothing of what he was feeling, he said curtly. 'Come in.'

It was Jenny.

'I emailed you the data you asked for.' She handed him a folder. 'But I know you like a hard copy as well.'

He nodded. 'Anything crop up while I was away?'

'Nothing major. There were a couple of problems with some of the pre-order sites, and the live stream was only working intermittently on Tuesday. But Ms Mason sorted them out so—'

Ram stiffened. 'Ms Mason? Why didn't you tell me she called?'

Jenny's eyes widened. 'Because she didn't call. She's here.'

He stared past her, his chest tightening with shock.

'Since when?'

'Since Monday.' She smiled. 'But she's leaving tonight. Oh, and she's pr—'

He cut her off. 'And nobody thought to tell me?' he demanded.

'I thought you knew. I— Is there a problem?' Jenny stammered. 'I thought she was still under contract.'

Blood was pounding in his ears.

Glancing at his secretary's scared expression, he shook his head and softened his voice. 'There isn't, and she is.'

He could hardly believe it. Nola was in the building and yet she hadn't bothered to come and find him.

As though reading his thoughts, Jenny gave him a small, anxious smile. 'She probably thinks you're still in New York. I'm sure she'd like to see you,' she said breathlessly.

Remembering the email Nola had sent him, he felt his pulse twitch. That seemed unlikely, but it wasn't her choice.

He smiled blandly. 'I'm sure she does. Maybe you could get her on the phone, Jenny, and tell her I'd like to see her in my office. When it's convenient, of course. It's just that we have some unfinished business.'

But it wasn't going to stay unfinished for long.

Watching the door close, he leaned back in his chair, his face expressionless.

Finally she was done!

Resting her forehead against the palms of her hands, Nola stifled a yawn. It might only be four o'clock in the afternoon, but it felt as if she'd worked an all-nighter. If only she could go back to bed. Really, though, what would be the point?

The fact she was sleeping badly was nothing to do with jet lag.

It was nerves.

She scowled. Not that she had any real reason to be nervous. Anna had been right—Ram was in New York on business. But that hadn't stopped the prickling sensation in the back of her neck as she'd walked into the RWI foyer, for even if the man himself wasn't in the building his presence was everywhere, making it impossible to shake off the feeling that there was still some link between them—an invisible bond that just wouldn't break.

Lowering her hands, she laid her fingers protectively over her stomach.

Not so invisible now.

For the last few weeks she'd been wearing her usual clothes, but today, for the first time, she'd struggled to get into her jeans. Fortunately she'd packed a pair of stretchy trousers that, although close-fitting, were more forgiving. She glanced down at her bump and smiled. It wasn't large, but she definitely looked pregnant now, and several people—mostly women—had noticed and congratulated her.

It was lovely, seeing their faces light up and finally being able to share this new phase of her life. But she would still be glad when it was all over and she could walk out through the huge

RWI doors for the last time. And not just because of Ram's ghostly presence in the building. It felt wrong that people she barely knew—people who worked for Ram—knew that she was pregnant when he didn't.

And somehow, being here in his building, telling herself that he wouldn't want to know about the baby or be a father, didn't seem to be working anymore. He *was* the father. And being here had made that fact unavoidable.

Thankfully her train of thought was interrupted as her phone rang. Glancing at the screen, she frowned, her stomach clenching involuntarily.

It was Ram's secretary, Jenny.

'Hi, Jenny. Is everything okay?

'Yes, everything's fine, Ms Mason. I was just ringing to ask if you'd mind popping up to the office? Mr Walker would like to see you.'

Mr Walker.

She opened her mouth to say some words, but no sound came from her lips.

'I thought he was away,' she managed finally. 'On business.'

'He was.' To her shell-shocked ears Jenny's voice sounded painfully bright and happy. 'But he flew back in this afternoon. And he particularly asked to see you. Apparently you have unfinished business?'

Nola nodded, too stunned by Jenny's words

even to register the fact that the other woman couldn't see her.

'Okay, well, he said to come up whenever it's convenient, so I'll see you in a bit.'

'Okay, see you then,' Nola lied.

As she hung up her heart began leaping like a salmon going upstream. For a moment she couldn't move, then slowly she closed her laptop and picked up her jacket.

Where could she go? Not her hotel. He might track her down. Nor the airport—at least not yet. No, probably it would be safest just to hide in some random café until it was time to check in.

On legs that felt like blancmange, she walked across the office and out into the corridor.

'Mr Walker? I'm just making some coffee. Can I get you anything?'

Ram looked up at Jenny.

'No, thank you, Jenny. I'm good.'

He glanced down at his phone and frowned. It was half past four. A flicker of apprehension ran down his spine.

'By the way, did you call Ms Mason?' he asked casually.

She nodded. 'Yes, and she said she'd be up in a bit.'

He nodded. 'Good. Excellent.'

He felt stupidly elated at her words, and suddenly so restless that he couldn't stay sitting at his desk a moment longer.

'Actually, I might just go and stretch my legs, Jenny. If Ms Mason turns up, ask her to wait in my office, please.'

The idea of Nola having to wait for him was strangely satisfying and, grabbing his jacket, he walked out through the door and began wandering down the corridor. Most of his staff were at their desks, but as he turned the corner into the large open-plan reception area he saw a group of people waiting for the lift.

Walking towards them, he felt a thrill of anticipation at the thought of finally seeing her again—and then abruptly he stopped dead, his eyes freezing with shock and disbelief. For there, standing slightly apart from the rest, her jacket folded over her arm, was Nola.

He watched, transfixed, as she stepped into the lift. Her long dark hair was coiled at the nape of her neck, and a tiny part of his brain registered that he'd never seen her wear it like that before.

But the bigger part was concentrating not on her hair but on the small, rounded, unmistakable bump of her stomach.

He heard his own sharp intake of breath as though from a long way away.

She was pregnant.

Pregnant.

A vice seemed to be closing around his throat. He felt like a drowning man watching his life play out in front of his eyes. A life that had just been derailed, knocked off course by a single night of passion.

And then, just as his legs overrode his brain, the lift doors closed and she was gone.

He stood gazing across the office, his head spinning, his breath scrabbling inside his chest like an animal trying to get out.

She was pregnant—several months pregnant at least—and frantically he rewound back through the calendar. But even before he reached the date when they'd slept together he knew that the baby could be his.

The blood seemed to drain from his body.

So why hadn't she said anything to him?

She'd been in the office for days. Yes, he'd been in New York when she arrived, but Jenny had spoken to her earlier. Nola knew he was in the building. Knew that he wanted to see her—

Remembering his remark about unfinished business, he almost laughed out loud.

Unfinished business.

You could say that again.

So why hadn't she said anything to him?

The question looped inside his head, each time growing louder and louder, like a car alarm. The obvious and most logical answer was that he was not the father.

Instantly he felt his chest tighten. The thought of Nola giving herself to another man made him want to smash his fists into the wall.

Surely she wouldn't—she couldn't have.

A memory rose up inside him, stark and unfiltered, of Nola, her body melting into his. She had been like fire under his skin. For that one night she had been his.

But was that baby his too?

A muscle flickered along the line of his jaw and he felt his anger curdle, swirling and separating into fury and frustration. Turning, he strode back into his office.

There was no way he could second-guess this. He had to know for certain.

'Tell Mike to bring the car round to the front of the building—*now*,' he barked at Jenny. 'I need to get to the airport.'

Ten minutes later he was slouched in the back of his limo. His head was beginning to clear finally, and now his anger was as cold and hostile as the arctic tundra.

How could she do this?

Treating him as if he didn't matter, as if he'd only had some walk-on part in her life. If he was the father, he should be centre stage.

His hands clenched in his lap. He hated the feeling of being sidelined, of being secondary to the key players in the drama, for it reminded him of his childhood, and the years he'd spent trying to fit into his parents' complex relationship.

But he wasn't a child anymore. He was man who might be about to have a child of his own.

His breath stilled in his throat.

Only *how* could he be the father? She had told him she was safe. But there was always an element of risk—particularly for a man like him, a man who would be expected to provide generous financial support for his child. Which was why he always used precautions of his own.

Except that night with Nola.

He'd wanted her so badly that he couldn't bring himself to do anything that might have risked them pausing, maybe changing their minds—like putting on a condom.

Feeling the car slow, he glanced up, his pulse starting to accelerate.

Was the baby his? He would soon find out.

Before the limo had even come to a stop, he was opening the door and stepping onto the pavement.

Dragging her suitcase through the airport, Nola frowned. She had waited as long as possible before arriving at the airport, and now she was worried she would be too late to check in her luggage.

But any worry she might be feeling now was

nothing to the stress of staying at the office. Knowing he was in the building had been unsettling enough, but the fact that Ram had asked to see her—

She didn't need to worry about that now and, curving her hand protectively over her stomach, she breathed out slowly, trying to calm herself as she stopped in front of the departures board.

She was just trying to locate her flight when there was some kind of commotion behind her and, turning, she saw that there was a crowd of people pointing and milling around.

'They're shooting a commercial,' the woman standing next to her said knowledgeably. 'It was in the paper. It's for beer. Apparently it's got that rugby player in it, and a crocodile.'

'A real one?'

The woman laughed. 'Yes, but it's not here. I just meant in the advert. I don't think they'd be allowed to bring a real croc to an airport. That'd be way too dangerous.'

Nodding politely, Nola smiled—and then she caught her breath for, striding towards her, his lean, muscular body parting the crowds like a mythical wind, and looking more dangerous than any wild animal, was Ram Walker.

nothing to the stress of arriving at the office
knowing he was there. She had been busy
thoroughly, but she had felt that Sam had asked to
see her

CHAPTER FIVE

As SHE WATCHED his broad shoulders cutting through the clumps of passengers like a scythe through wheat Nola couldn't move. Or speak, or even think. Shock seemed to have robbed her of the ability to do anything but gape.

And as he made his way across the departures lounge towards her she couldn't decide if it was shock or desire that was making her heart feel as if it was about to burst.

Mind numb, she stood frozen, like a movie on pause. It was just over three months since she'd last seen him. Three months of trying and failing to forget the man who had changed her life completely.

She'd assumed she just needed more time, that eventually his memory would fade. Only now he was here, and she knew she'd been kidding herself. She would never forget Ram—and not just because she was pregnant with his baby.

Her body began to shake, and instinctively she folded her arms over her stomach.

A baby he didn't even know existed.

A baby she had deliberately chosen to conceal from him.

And just like that she knew his being here

wasn't some cosmic coincidence: he was coming to find her.

Before that thought had even finished forming in her head he was there, standing in front of her, and suddenly she wished she was sitting down, for the blazing anger in his grey gaze almost knocked her off her feet.

'Going somewhere?' he asked softly.

She had forgotten his voice. Not the sound of it, but the power it had to throw her into a state of confusion, to turn her emotions into a swirling mass of chaos that made even breathing a challenge.

Looking up at him, hoping that her voice was steadier than her heartbeat, she said hoarsely, 'Mr Walker. I wasn't expecting to see you.'

He didn't reply. For a moment his narrowed gaze stayed fixed on her face, and then her skin seemed to blister and burn as slowly his eyes slid down over her throat and breast, stopping pointedly on the curve of her stomach.

'Yes, it's been a day of surprises all round.'

His heart crashing against his ribs, Ram stared at Nola in silence. He had spent the last two hours waiting at the check-in desk for her, his nerves buzzing beneath his skin at the sight of every long-haired brunette. At first when she hadn't turned up he'd been terrified that she'd caught another flight. But finally it had dawned on him that she was probably just hoping to avoid him, and therefore was going to arrive at the last minute.

Now that she was here, he was struggling to come to terms with what he could see—for seeing her in the office had been such a shock that he'd almost started to think that maybe what he'd seen might not even have been real. After all, it had only been a glimpse...

Maybe it had been another woman with dark hair, and after months of thinking and dreaming about her he'd just imagined it was Nola.

Now, though, there could be no doubt, no confusion.

It was Nola, and she was pregnant.

But that didn't mean he was the father.

He felt himself jerk forward—doubt and then certainty vibrating through his bones.

If that baby was another man's child, he knew she would have met his gaze proudly. Instead she looked hunted, cornered, like a small animal facing a predator it couldn't outrun.

In other words, guilty as hell.

With an effort he shifted his gaze from her stomach to her face. Her lips were pale, and her blue eyes were huge and uncomprehending. She looked, if possible, more stunned than he felt. But right now feelings were secondary to the truth.

'So this is why you've been giving me the runaround?' he asked slowly. 'I suppose I should offer my congratulations.' He paused, letting the silence stretch between them. *'To both of us.'*

Watching her eyes widen with guilt, he felt new shoots of anger pushing up inside him, so that suddenly his pulse was too fast and irregular.

'I wonder—when, exactly, were you going to tell me you were pregnant?'

Looking up into his face, Nola felt her breath jerk in her throat. He was angrier than she'd ever seen him. Angrier than she'd ever seen anyone. And he had every right to be.

Had she been standing there, confronted by both this truth and the months of deception that had preceded it, she would have felt as furious and thwarted as he did. But somehow knowing that made her feel more defensive, for that was only half the story. The half that *didn't* include her reasons for acting as she had.

Lifting her chin, she met his gaze. 'Why would I tell you I'm pregnant? As of twenty minutes ago, I don't actually work for you anymore.'

Her hands curled up into fists in front of her as he took a step towards her.

'Don't play games with me, Nola.'

His eyes burned into hers, and the raw hostility in his voice suffocated her so that suddenly she could hardly breathe.

'And don't pretend this has got anything to with your employment rights. You're having a baby, and we both know it could be mine. So you should have told me.'

Around her, the air sharpened. She could feel people turning to stare at them curiously.

Forcing herself to hold his gaze, she glared at him. 'This has got nothing to do with you.'

A nerve pulsed along his jawline.

'And you want me to take your word for that, do you?' He gazed at her in naked disbelief. 'On the basis of what? Your outstanding display of honesty up until now?'

She blinked. 'You don't know for certain if you're the father,' she said quickly, failing to control the rush of colour to her face.

His eyes locked onto hers, and instantly she felt the tension in her spine tighten like a guy rope.

'No. But *you* do.'

She flinched, wrong-footed.

How was this happening?

Not him finding her. It would have been a matter of moments for his secretary to check her flight time. But why was he here? Over the last three months she'd spent hours imagining this moment, playing out every possible type of scenario. In not one of them had he pursued her to the airport and angrily demanded the truth.

Her heart began to pound fiercely.

It would be tempting to think that he cared about the baby.

Tempting, but foolish.

Ram's appearance at the airport, his frustration and anger, had nothing to do with any sudden rush of paternal feelings on his part. Understandably, he hadn't liked finding out second-hand that she was pregnant. But that didn't mean he could just turn up and start throwing his weight around.

'I don't see why you're making this into such a big deal,' she snapped. 'We both know that you have absolutely no interest in being a father anyway.'

Ram studied her face, his pulse beating slow and hard.

It was true that up until this moment, he'd believed that fatherhood was not for him. But he'd been talking about a concept, a theoretical child, and Nola knew that as well as he did.

His chest tightened with anger.

'That doesn't mean I don't want to know *when* I am going to be one. In fact, I think I have a right to know. However, if you're saying that you really don't know who the father is, then I suggest we find out for certain.' His eyes held hers. 'I believe it's a fairly simple test. Of course it would mean you'd have to miss your flight…'

Imprisoned by his dark grey gaze, Nola gritted her teeth.

He was calling her bluff, and she hated him for it.

But what she hated more was the fact that in spite of her anger and resentment she could feel her body unfurling inside, as though it was waking from a long hibernation. And even though he was causing mayhem in her life, her longing for him still sucked the breath from her lungs.

Glancing at his profile, she felt a pulse of heat that had nothing to do with anger skim over her skin. But right now the stupid, senseless way she reacted to Ram didn't matter. All she cared about was catching that plane—and that was clearly not going to happen unless Ram found out, one way or another, if this baby was his.

So why not just tell him the truth?

Squaring her shoulders, she met his gaze. 'Fine,' she said slowly. 'You're the father.'

She didn't really know how she'd expected him to react, but he didn't say or do anything. He just continued to stare at her impassively, his grey eyes dark and unblinking.

'I know you don't want to be involved, and that's fine. I'm not expecting you to be,' she said quickly. 'That's one of the reasons I didn't tell you.'

'So you had more than one reason, then?' he said quietly.

She frowned, unsure of how she should respond. But she didn't get a chance to reply, for as though he had suddenly become conscious of the sidelong glances and the sudden stillness surrounding them, he reached down and picked up her suitcase.

'I suggest we finish this in private.'

Turning, Ram walked purposefully across the departures lounge. Inside his head, though, he had no idea where he was going. Or what to do when he got there.

You're the father!

Three words he'd never expected or wanted to hear.

Then—*boom!*—there they were, blowing apart his carefully ordered world.

His chest grew tight. Only this wasn't just about his life anymore; there was a new life to consider now.

Through the haze of his confused thoughts he noticed two empty chairs in the corner, next to a vending machine, and gratefully sat down in one.

His head was spinning. Seeing Nola pregnant at the office, he'd guessed that he might be the father. But it had been just that. A guess. It hadn't felt real—not least because he'd spent all his life believing that this moment would never happen.

Only now it had, and he would have expected his response to be a mix of resentment and regret.

But, incredibly, what he was actually feeling was resolve. A determination to be part of his child's life.

Now all he needed to do was persuade Nola of that fact.

Glancing over to where Ram now sat, with that familiar shuttered look on his handsome face, Nola felt resentment surge through her. How could he do this? Just stroll back into her life and take over, expecting her to follow him across the room like some puppy he was training?

He had said he wanted to know the truth and so she'd told him, hoping that would be the end of their conversation. Why, then, did they need to speak in private? What else was there to say?

Her eyes narrowed. Maybe she should just leave him sitting there. Leave the airport, catch a train, or just go and hide in some nameless hotel. Show Ram that she wasn't going to be pushed around by him.

But clearly he was determined to have the last word, and trying to stop him doing so would be like trying to defy gravity: exhausting, exasperating, and ultimately futile.

The fact was that he was just so much more relentless than she could ever be, and whatever it was that drove his desire—no, his determination to win, she couldn't compete with it. Whether she liked it or not, this conversation was going to have to happen, so she might as well get on with it or she would never get on that plane.

Mutinously, she walked over to him and, ignoring the small satisfied smile on his face, sat down next to him.

Around her people were moving, picking up luggage and chatting, happy to be going home or going on holiday, and for a split second she wished with an intensity that almost doubled her over that it was her and Ram going away together. That she could rewind time, meet him in some other way, under different circumstances, and—

Her lip curled.

And what?

She and Ram might share a dizzying sexual chemistry, but there was no trust, no honesty and no harmony. Most of their conversations ended up in an argument, and the only time they'd managed to stay on speaking terms was when they hadn't needed to speak.

Remembering the silence between them in the lift, the words left unspoken on her lips as he'd covered her mouth with his, she felt heat break out on her skin.

That night had been different. That night all the tension and antagonism between them had melted into the darkness and they had melted into one another, their quickening bodies hot and liquid…

She swallowed.

But sex wasn't enough to sustain a relationship. And one night of passion, however incredible, wasn't going to make her change her mind. It had been a hard decision to make, but it was the right one. A two-parent set-up might be traditional—desirable, even—but not if one of those parents was always halfway out through the door, literally and emotionally.

Breathing out slowly, she turned her head and stared into his eyes. 'Look, what happened three months ago has got nothing to do with now...' She paused. 'It wasn't planned—we just made a mistake.'

For a moment, his gaze held hers, and then slowly he shook his head.

'We didn't make a mistake, Nola.'

'I wasn't talking about the baby,' she said quickly.

His eyes rested intently on her face.

'Neither was I.'

And just like that she felt her stomach flip over, images from the night they'd spent together exploding inside her head like popping corn. Suddenly her whole body was quivering, and it was all she could do not to lean over and kiss him, to give in to that impulse to taste and touch that beautiful mouth once again—

Taking a quick breath, she dragged her eyes away from him, ignoring the sparks scattering over her skin.

'You said you wanted to finish this, Ram, but

we can't,' she said hoarsely. 'Because it never started. It was just a one-night stand, remember?'

'Oh, I remember every single moment of that night. As I'm sure you do, Nola.'

His eyes gleamed, and instantly her pulse began to accelerate.

'But this isn't about just one night anymore. Our one-night stand has got long-term consequences.' He gestured towards her stomach.

'But not for you.' She looked up at him stubbornly, her blue eyes wide with frustration. 'Whatever connection we had, it ended a long time ago.'

'Given that you're pregnant with my child, that would seem to be a little premature and counterintuitive,' he said softly. 'But I don't think there's anything to be gained by continuing this discussion now.' He grimaced. 'Or here. I suggest we leave it for a day or two. I can take you back to the city—I have an apartment there you can use as a base—and I'll talk to my lawyers, get some kind of intermediate financial settlement set up.'

Nola gazed at him blankly.

Apartment? Financial settlement?

What was he talking about?

This wasn't about money. This was about what was best for their child, and Ram was *not* father material. A father should be consistent, compassionate, and capable of making personal sacrifices for the sake of his child. But Ram was just not suited to making the kinds of commitment and sacrifices expected and required by parenthood.

She had no doubt that financially he would be generous, but children needed more than money. They needed to be loved. To be wanted.

Memories of her own father and his lack of interest filled her head, and suddenly she couldn't meet Ram's eyes. Her father had been a workaholic. For him, business had come first, and if he'd had any time and energy left after a working day he'd chosen to spend it either out entertaining clients or with one of his many mistresses. Home-life, his wife and his daughter, had been right at the bottom of his agenda—more like a footnote, in fact.

Being made to feel so unimportant had blighted her childhood. As an adult, too, she had struggled to believe in herself. It had taken a long time, her friendship with Anna, and a successful career to overcome that struggle. And it was a struggle she was determined her child would never have to face.

But what was the point of telling Ram any of that? He wouldn't understand. How could he? It was not as if he'd ever doubted himself or felt that he wasn't good enough.

'No,' she said huskily. 'That's not going to happen.' She was shaking her head but her eyes were fixed on his face. 'I don't want your money, Ram, or your apartment. And I'm sorry if this offends your *romantic sensibilities*, but I don't want you in my baby's life just because we spent eight hours on a sofa in your office.'

Recognising his own words, Ram felt a swirling, incoherent fury surge up inside him. Wrong, he thought savagely. She had *belonged* to him that night, and now she was carrying his baby part of her would belong to him for ever.

Leaning back, he let his eyes roam over her face, his body responding with almost primeval force to her flushed cheeks and resentful pout even as his mind plotted his next move.

What mattered most was keeping her in Australia, and losing his temper would only make her more determined to leave. So, reining in his anger, he stretched out his legs and gazed at her calmly.

'Sadly for you, that decision is not yours to make. I'm not a lawyer, but I'm pretty sure that it's paternity, not romantic sensibilities, that matters to a judge. But why don't you call your lawyer just to make sure?'

It wasn't true but judging by the flare of fear in her eyes, Nola's knowledge of parental rights was clearly based on law procedural dramas not legal expertise. Nola could hardly breathe. Panic was strangling her. Why was he suddenly talking about lawyers and judges?

'Wh-Why are you doing this?' she stammered. 'I know you're angry with me for not telling you about the baby, and I understand that. But you have to understand that you're the reason I didn't say anything.'

'Oh, I see. So it's *my* fault you didn't tell me?'

He was speaking softly, but there was no mistaking the dangerous undertone curling through his words.

'*My* fault that you deliberately chose to avoid me at the office today? And I suppose it'll be my fault, too, when my child grows up without a father and spends the rest of his life feeling responsible—'

He broke off, his face hardening swiftly.

She bit her lip. 'No, of course not. I just meant that from everything you said before I didn't think you'd want to know. So I made a choice.'

Ram could hear the slight catch in her voice but he ignored it. Whatever he'd said before was irrelevant now. This baby was real. And it was his. Besides, nothing he'd said in the past could excuse her lies and deceit.

'And that's what this is about, is it? *Your* choices? *Your* pregnancy? *Your* baby?' He shook his head. 'This is not *your* baby, Nola, it's *our* baby—mine as much as yours—and you know it. And I am going be a part of his or her life.'

Nola stared at him numbly, her head pounding

in time with her heart. She didn't know what to say to him—hadn't got the words to defend herself or argue her case. Not that it mattered. He wasn't listening to her anyway.

Shoulders back, neck tensing, she looked away, her eyes searching frantically for some way to escape—and then her heart gave a jolt as she suddenly saw the time on the departures board.

The next second she had snatched her suitcase and was on her feet, pulse racing.

'What do you think you're doing?'

Ram was standing in front of her, blocking her way.

'I have to go!'

Her voice was rising, and a couple of people turned to look at her. But she didn't care. If she missed this flight she would be stuck in Sydney for hours, possibly days, and she had to get away—as far away from Ram as quickly as she could.

'They've called my flight so I need to check in my luggage.'

For a moment he stared at her in silence, and then his face shifted and, leaning forward, he plucked the suitcase handle from her fingers.

'Let me take that!'

He strode away from her and, cursing under her breath, she hurried after him.

'I really don't need your help,' she said through gritted teeth.

Tucking the suitcase under his arm, he smiled blandly. 'Of course not. But you have to understand I don't fly commercial, so all this rushing around is very exciting for me. It's actually better than watching a film.'

He sounded upbeat—buoyant, almost—and she glowered at him, part baffled, part exasperated by this sudden change in mood.

'That's wonderful, Ram,' she said sarcastically. 'But I'm not here to be your entertainment for the evening.'

'If you were my entertainment for the evening you wouldn't be getting breathless from running around an airport,' he said softly. And, reaching over, he took her arm and pulled her towards him.

Her breath stuttered in her throat, and suddenly all her senses were concentrated on his hand and on the firmness of his grip and the heat of his skin through the fabric of her shirt.

'You need to slow down. You're pregnant. And besides…' he gestured towards the seemingly endless queue of people looping back and forth across the width of the room '…I don't think a couple of minutes is going to make that much difference.'

Gazing at the queue, Nola groaned. 'I'm never going to make it.'

'You don't know that.' Ram frowned. 'Why don't we ask at the desk?'

He pointed helpfully to where two women in uniform were chatting with a group of passengers surrounded by trolleys and toddlers. But Nola was already hurrying across the room.

'Excuse me. Could you help me, please? I'm supposed to be on this flight to Edinburgh but I need to check in my baggage.'

Handing over her boarding pass, she held her breath as the woman glanced down at it, and then back at her screen, before finally shaking her head.

'I'm sorry, the bag drop desk is closed—and even if we rush you through it's a good ten minutes to get to the boarding gate.' She grimaced. 'And, looking ahead, all Edinburgh flights are full for the next twenty-four hours. You might be able to pick up a cancellation, but that would mean hanging around at the airport. I'm sorry I can't be more helpful...'

'That's okay,' Nola said stiffly. 'It's really not your fault.'

And it wasn't.

Turning away, she stalked over to where Ram stood, watching her unrepentantly.

'This is your fault,' she snapped. 'If you hadn't been talking to me I'd have heard it when they called my flight and then I would have checked in my luggage on time.'

He gazed at her blandly. 'Oh, was that your

flight to Edinburgh? I didn't realise it was that important. Like I said, I don't fly commercial, so—'

Nola stared at him, wordless with disbelief, her nails cutting into her hands. 'Don't give me that "I don't fly commercial" rubbish. You knew exactly what you were doing.'

He smiled down at her serenely. 'Really? You think I'd deliberately and selfishly withhold a vital piece of information?' He shook his head, his eyes glittering. 'I'm shocked. I mean, who would *do* something like that?'

She was shaking with anger. 'This is not the same at all.'

'No, it's not,' he said softly. 'I stopped you catching a flight, and you tried to stop me finding out I was a father.'

'But I didn't do it to hurt you,' she said shakily. 'Or to punish you.

And she hadn't—only how could she prove that to Ram? How could she explain to him that she had only been trying to prevent her child's future from inheriting her past? How could she tell him that life had taught her that no father was better than a bad father.

She shivered. It was all such a mess. And she didn't know what to do to fix it. All she knew was that she wanted to go home. To be anywhere but at this noisy, crowded airport, standing in front of a man who clearly hated her.

Her eyes were stinging and she turned away blindly.

'Nola. Don't go.'

Something in his voice stopped her, and slowly, reluctantly, she met his gaze.

He was staring at her impassively, his eyes cool and detached.

'Look, I don't think either of us was expecting to have this conversation, and even though I think we both know that we have a lot to talk about we need time and privacy to do it properly. I also know that I need to get home, and you need a plane. So why don't you borrow mine?'

She looked at him dazedly. 'Borrow your plane?'

He nodded. 'I have a private jet. Just sitting there, all ready to go, thirty minutes from here. It's got a proper bedroom and a bathroom. Two, in fact, so you can get a proper night's sleep. I guess I *am* responsible in part for making you miss your flight, so it's really the least I can do.'

He looked so handsome, so contrite, and clearly he wanted to make amends. Besides, all her other options involved an effort she just couldn't summon up the energy to make right now.

Biting her lip, she nodded.

Exactly thirty-three minutes later, Ram's limo turned into a private airfield.

As the car slid to a halt, Nola glanced over to

where Ram sat gazing out of the window in silence. 'Thank you for letting me use your plane,' she said carefully.

Turning, he looked over at her, his eyes unreadable in the gloom of the car.

'My pleasure. I called ahead and told the pilot where to take you, so you can just sit back and enjoy the ride.'

She nodded, her heart contracting guiltily as his words replayed inside her head. He was being so reasonable—kind, even—and like a storm that had blown itself out the tension between them had vanished.

Her pulse was racing. A few hours earlier she'd been desperate to leave the country, to get away from Ram. Only now that it was finally time to go something was holding her back, making her hesitate, just as she had three months ago when she'd crept out of his office in the early hours of the morning. It was the same feeling—a feeling that somehow she was making a mistake.

She held her breath. But staying was not an option. She needed to go home, even if that meant feeling guilty. Only she hadn't expected to mind so much.

Her heart was bumping inside her chest like a bird trapped in a room and, clearing her throat, she said quickly, 'I was wrong not to tell you about the baby. I should have done, and I'm sorry. I know we've got an awful lot to discuss. But you're right—we do need time and privacy to talk about it properly, so thank you for being so understanding about me leaving.'

His eyes were light and relaxed, and she felt another pang beneath her heart.

'I'm glad you agree, and I feel sure we'll see each other very soon.'

The walk from the car to the plane seemed to last for ever, but finally she was smiling at the young, male flight attendant who had stepped forward to greet her.

'Good evening, Ms Mason, welcome on board. My name is Tom, and I'll be looking after you on this flight with my colleagues, James and Megan. If you need anything, please just ask.'

Collapsing into a comfortable armchair that bore no resemblance to the cramped seats on every other flight she'd ever been on, she tried not to let herself look out of the window. But finally she could bear it no more and, turning her head, she glanced down at the tarmac.

It was deserted. The limo was gone.

Swallowing down the sudden small, hard lump of misery in her throat, she sat back and watched numbly as Tom brought her some iced water and a selection of magazines.

'If you could just put on your seatbelt, Ms Mason, we'll be taking off in a couple of minutes.'

'Yes, of course.'

Leaning back, she closed her eyes and listened to the hum of the air conditioning, and then finally she heard the engines start to whine.

'Is this seat taken?'

A male voice. Deep and very familiar.

But it couldn't be him—

Her eyes snapped open and her heart began to thump, for there, staring down at her, with something very like a smile tugging at his mouth, was Ram.

She stared up at him in confusion. 'What are you doing here?'

'I thought you might like some company.'

Company! She frowned. Glancing past him at the window, she could see that they were starting to move forward, and across the cabin Tom and his colleagues were buckling themselves into their seats.

'I don't think there's time,' she said hurriedly. 'We're just about to take off.'

He shrugged. 'Well, like you said, we do have an awful lot to talk about.'

A trickle of cool air ran down her spine, and she felt a pang of uneasiness.

'Yes, but not now—'

She broke off as he dropped into the seat beside her.

'Why not now?' Sliding his belt across his lap,

he stretched out his long legs. 'Just the two of us on a private jet…'

Pausing, he met her gaze, and the steady intensity of his grey eyes made the blood stop moving in her veins.

'Surely this is the perfect opportunity!'

CHAPTER SIX

NOLA STARED AT him uncertainly. Beneath the sound of her heartbeat she heard the plane's wheels starting to rumble across the tarmac. But she barely registered it. Instead, her brain was frantically trying to make sense of his words.

He couldn't possibly be intending to fly to Scotland with her, so it must be his idea of a joke.

Glancing up into his face, she felt her breath catch.

Except that he didn't look as if he was joking.

Taking a deep breath, trying to appear calmer than she felt, she forced herself to smile. 'I couldn't ask you to do that,' she said lightly. 'It's not as if it's on your way home.'

His grey gaze rested on her face. 'But you're not asking me, are you? Nor am I asking *you*, as it happens.'

Her face felt stiff with shock and confusion. Slowly she shook her head. 'But this isn't what we agreed. You said I could borrow your plane—you didn't say anything about coming with me.'

He gazed at her blandly. 'I thought you said we had a lot to talk about.'

'You know I didn't mean *now*.' Her voice rose. This was madness. Total and utter madness.

Except madness implied that Ram was acting irrationally, and there was nothing random or illogical about his decision to join her on the plane. He was simply proving a point, and getting his own way just like he always did.

She felt as though she was going to throw up.

'You tricked me. You made me miss my flight and then you offered to let me use your plane just so you could trap me here.'

And, fool that she was, she had actually believed he was trying to make amends.

Her heart began to pound fiercely. Not only that, she'd apologised to him. *Apologised* for not telling him about the baby and *thanked* him for being so understanding.

But everything he'd said had been a lie.

How could she have been so stupid—so gullible?

Her cheeks felt as if they were on fire. 'Why are you doing this to me?' she whispered.

He shrugged. 'It was your choice. I didn't make you do anything. You could have waited for a regular flight.' His mouth hardened. 'Except that would have meant talking to me. So I made a calculated guess that you'd do pretty much anything to avoid that—including accepting the offer of a no-strings flight back to Scotland.'

'Except there *are* strings, aren't there?' she snapped. 'Like the fact that you never said you were coming with me.'

He looked at her calmly. 'Well, I thought it might be a little counterproductive.'

Her pulse was crashing in her ears. 'I can't believe you're doing this,' she said hoarsely.

Leaning forward, he picked up one of the magazines and began flicking casually through the pages. 'Then you clearly don't know me as well as you thought you did.' He smiled at her serenely. 'But don't worry. Now that we have the chance to spend some time alone, I'm sure we'll get to know each other a whole lot better.'

Her hands clenched in her lap. She was breathless with anger and frustration. 'But you can't just hijack this plane—'

'Given that it's my plane, I'd say that would be almost impossible,' he agreed.

'I don't care that it's your plane. People don't behave like this. It's insane!'

'Oh, I don't think so.' He gazed at her steadily. 'You're pregnant with my child, Nola. Insane would be letting you fly off into the sunset with just your word that you'll get in touch.'

'So you just decided to come with me to the other side of the world?' she snapped. 'Yeah, I can see that's *really* rational.'

For a moment she glared at him in silence, and then her pulse began to jerk erratically over her skin, like a needle skipping across a record, as he leaned over and rested his hand lightly on the smooth mound of her stomach.

'Whether you like it or not, Nola, this baby is mine too. And until we get this sorted out I'm not letting you out of my sight. Where you go, I go.'

Blood was roaring in her ears. On one level his words made no sense, for she hardly knew him. He was a stranger, and what they'd shared amounted to so little. The briefest of flings. A night on a sofa.

And yet so much had happened in that one night. Not just the baby, but the fire between them—a storm of passion that had left her breathless and dazed, and eclipsed every sexual experience she'd had or would ever have.

She'd known that night that a part of her would always belong to Ram. She just hadn't realised then that it would turn out to be a baby. But now that he knew the truth was anything he'd done really that big a surprise? She was carrying his child, and she knew enough about Ram to know that he would never willingly give up control of anything that belonged to him.

Still, that didn't give him the right to trap her and manipulate her like this, bending her to his will as though being pregnant made her an extension of his life.

'You didn't have to do this,' she said hoarsely. 'I told you I was going to get in touch and I would have done.'

'I've saved you the trouble, then.' He gave her a small, taunting smile. 'It's okay—you don't need to thank me.'

She glowered at him in silence, her brain seething as she tried to think up some slick comeback that would puncture his overdeveloped ego.

But, really, why bother? Whatever she said wasn't going to change the fact that they were stuck with each other for the foreseeable future.

Only just because he'd managed to trick her into getting on his plane, it didn't mean that he was going to have everything his own way. Remembering his remark back at the airport, she felt her breathing jerk, and she curled her fingers into the palms of her hands. She sure as hell wasn't going to spend the rest of this flight entertaining him.

'I'd love to keep on chatting,' she said coldly. 'But it's been a long, and exhausting day, and as you can imagine I'm very tired.'

Their eyes met—his calm and appraising, hers combative—and there was a short, taut silence.

Finally he shrugged. 'Of course. I'll show you to your room.'

Her room!

'No—' She lurched back in her seat.

She would have liked to brush her teeth, and maybe put on something more comfortable, but the thought of undressing within a five-mile radius of Ram made her heart start to beat painfully fast.

'Actually, I think I'd rather stay here,' she said quickly. 'These seats recline, don't they? And I'm not really sleeping properly at the moment anyway.'

He stared at her speculatively, and she wondered if he was going to demand that she use the bedroom.

But after a moment, he simply nodded. 'I'll get you a blanket.'

Five minutes later, tucked cosily beneath a soft cashmere blanket, Nola tilted back her seat and turned her head pointedly away from where Ram sat beside her, working on his laptop.

How was he able to do any work anyway? she thought irritably. After everything that had happened in the last few hours anybody else—her included—would have been too distracted, too agitated, too exhausted.

But then wasn't that one of the reasons she'd been so reluctant to tell him about the baby? Just like her father, he always put business first, pleasure second, and then the boring nitty-gritty of domestic life last. And, having offered to fly her home in his private jet, he probably thought he'd been generous enough—caring, even.

Stifling a yawn, she closed her eyes. Ram's deluded world view didn't matter to her any more than he did. He might have been her boss, and he might be calling the shots now. But that would change as soon as they landed in Scotland. Edinburgh was her home, and she wasn't about to let anyone—especially not Ram Walker—trample over the life she had built there. Feeling calmer, she burrowed further down beneath the blanket...

She woke with a start.

For a moment she lay there, utterly disorientated, trying to make sense of the soft wool brushing against her face and the clean coolness of the air, and then suddenly she was wide awake as the previous night's events slid into place inside her head.

Opening her eyes, she struggled to sit up, her senses on high alert.

Why did it feel as though they were slowing down? Surely she couldn't have slept for that long? Picking up her phone, she glanced at the screen and frowned. It didn't make sense. They'd only been flying a couple of hours, and yet the plane seemed to be descending.

'Good, you're awake.'

Her heart gave a jolt, and she turned.

It was Ram. He was standing beside her, his face calm, his grey eyes watching her with an expression she didn't quite recognise.

'I thought I was going to have to wake you,' he said coolly.

He was holding his laptop loosely in one hand, so he must have spent the last few hours working, and yet he looked just as though he'd had a full eight hours' sleep. She could practically feel the energy humming off him like a force field.

But that wasn't the only reason her pulse was racing.

With his dark hair falling over his forehead, and his crisp white shirt hugging the muscles of his chest and arms, he looked like a movie star playing a CEO. Even the unflattering overhead lights did nothing to diminish his beauty.

Was it really necessary or fair for him to be that perfect? she thought desperately. Particularly when her own body seemed incapable of co-ordinating with her brain, so that despite his appalling behaviour at the airport her senses were responding shamelessly to his blatant masculinity.

Gritting her teeth, hoping that none of her thoughts were showing on her face, she met his gaze.

'Why are we slowing down? Are we stopping for fuel?'

'Something like that.'

He studied her face for a moment, and then glanced back along the cabin. 'I just need to go and speak to the crew. I won't be long.'

Biting her lip, she stared after him, a prickle spreading over her skin. She sat in uneasy silence, her senses tracking the plane's descent, until she felt the jolt as it landed.

Something felt a bit off. But probably it was just because she'd never flown on a private jet before. Usually at this point everyone would be standing up and pulling down their luggage, chatting and grabbing their coats. This was so quiet, so smooth, so civilised. So A-list.

Glancing out of the window, Nola smiled. They might not be in Scotland yet, but the weather was doing its best to make her feel as if they were. She could hear the wind already, and fat drops of rain were slapping against the glass.

'Come on—let's go!'

Turning, she saw that Ram was standing beside her, his hand held out towards her.

She frowned. 'Go where? Don't we just wait?'

'They need to clean the plane and do safety checks. And then the crew are going off-shift.'

She gazed up at him warily.

'So where are we going?'

'Somewhere more comfortable. It's not far.'

Her heart began to thump. Maybe it would have been better after all if she'd just waited for another flight. But it was too late to worry about that now.

It was warm outside—tropical, even—but she still ducked her head against the wind and the rain.

'Be careful.'

Ram took hold of her arm and, ignoring her protests, guided her down the stairs.

'I can manage,' she said curtly.

But still he ignored her, tightening his grip as he walked her across the runway to an SUV that was idling in the darkness.

Inside the car, he leaned forward and tapped against the glass. 'Thanks, Carl. Just take it slow, okay?'

'I thought you said it wasn't far,' she said accusingly.

Turning back to face her, he shrugged. But there was a small, satisfied smile on his handsome face that made her heart start to bang against her ribs.

'It isn't. But this way we stay nice and dry.' His eyes mocked her. 'Despite what you may have heard, I can't actually control the weather.'

She nodded, but she was barely listening to what he said; she was too busy squinting through the window into the darkness outside.

Stopover destinations to and from Australia usually depended on the airline. It could be Hong Kong, Dubai, Singapore or Los Angeles. Of course flying on a private jet probably meant that some of those options weren't available. But, even so, something didn't feel right.

For a start there were no lights, nor even anything that really passed as a building. In fact she couldn't really see much at all, except a tangled, dark mass of trees and vegetation stretching away into the distance. Her heart began to beat faster, and she felt a rush of cold air on her skin that had nothing to do with the car's air conditioning.

She forced herself to speak. 'Where exactly are we?'

'Queensland—just west of Cairns.'

Turning, she stared at him in confusion, her mouth suddenly dry.

'What? We haven't even left Australia? So why have we stopped? We're never going to get to Scotland at this rate!'

'We're not going to Scotland,' he said quietly.

That prickling feeling had returned, and with it a sensation that she was floating—that if she hadn't been gripping the door handle so tightly she might have just drifted away.

'What do you mean? Of course, we're going to Scotland—' She broke off as he started to shake his head.

'Actually, we're not.'

His eyes glittered in the darkness, and she felt her breath catch in her throat.

'We never were. It was always my intention to bring you here.'

She stared at him in silence. Fury, shock, disbelief and frustration were washing over her like waves breaking against a sea wall.

Here? Here!

What was he talking about?

'There is no *"here",'* she said shakily. 'We're in the middle of nowhere.'

He was mad. Completely mad. There was no other explanation for his behaviour. How could she not have noticed before?

'You and I need to talk, Nola.'

'And you want to do that in the middle of a jungle?' She was practically shouting now. Not that he seemed to care.

She watched in disbelief as calmly he shook his head.

'It's actually a rainforest. Only parts of it are classified as a jungle. And clearly I'm not expecting us to talk there. I have a house about three miles from here. It's very beautiful and completely private—what you might call secluded, in fact, so we won't be disturbed.'

Her head was spinning.

'I don't care if you have a palace with its own zoological gardens. I am not going there now or at any other time—and I'm definitely not going there with *you*.'

He lounged back against the seat, completely unperturbed by her outburst, his dark eyes locking onto hers. 'And yet here you are.'

She stared at him in shock, too stunned, too dazed to speak. Then, slowly, she started to shake her head. 'No. You can't do this. I want you to turn this car around now—'

Her whole body was shaking. This was far, far worse than missing her flight or Ram joining her on the plane.

Leaning forward, she began banging desperately on the glass behind the driver's head.

'Please—you have to help me!'

Behind her, she heard Ram sigh. 'You're going to hurt your hand, and it won't make any difference. So why don't you just calm down and try and relax?'

Her head jerked round. 'Relax! How am I supposed to relax? You're *kidnapping* me!'

Ram stretched out his legs. He could hear the exasperation and fury in her voice—could almost see it crackling from the ends of her gleaming dark hair.

Good, he thought silently. Now she knew how he felt. How it felt to have your life turned upside down. Suddenly no longer to be in charge of your own destiny.

'Am I? I'm not asking anyone for a ransom. Nor am I planning to blindfold you and tie you to the bed,' he said softly, his gaze holding hers. 'Unless, of course, you want me to.'

He watched two flags of colour rise on her cheekbones as she slid back into her seat, as far from him as was physically possible.

'All I want is for you to stop acting like some caveman.' She breathed out shakily. 'People don't behave like this. It's barbaric…primitive.'

'Primitive?' He repeated the word slowly, letting the seconds crawl by, feeling his groin hardening as she refused to make eye contact with him. 'I thought you liked primitive,' he said softly.

'That was different.' Turning her head sharply, she glowered at him. 'And it has nothing to do with any of this.'

'On the contrary. You and I tearing each other's clothes off has everything to do with this.'

'I don't want to talk about it,' she snapped, her blue eyes wide with fury. 'I don't want to talk to you about anything. In fact the only conversation I'm going to be having is with the police.'

She sounded breathless, as though she'd been running. He watched her pull out her phone and punch at the buttons.

'Oh, perhaps I should have mentioned it earlier… there's pretty much zero coverage out here.'

He smiled in a way that made her want to throw the phone at his head.

'It's one of the reasons I like it so much—no interruptions, no distractions.'

Fingers trembling with anger, she switched off her phone and pressed herself against the door. 'I hate you.'

'I don't care.'

The rest of the journey passed in uncomfortable silence. Nola felt as though she'd swallowed a bucket of ice; her whole body was rigid with cold, bitter fury. When finally the car came to a stop at his house she slid across the seat and out of the door without so much as acknowledging his presence.

Staring stonily at his broad shoulders in his dark suit jacket, she followed him through a series of rooms and corridors, barely registering anything other than the resentment hardening inside her chest.

'This is your room. The bathroom is through there.'

She glared at him. 'My room? How long are you planning on keeping me here?'

He ignored her. 'You'll find everything you need.'

'Really? You mean there's a shotgun and a shovel?'

His eyes hardened. 'The sooner you stop fighting me, Nola, the sooner this will all be over. If you need me, I'm just next door. I'll see you in the morning.'

'Unless you're going to lock me in, I won't be here in the morning.'

He stared at her impatiently. 'I don't need to lock you in. It would take you the best part of a day to walk back to the airfield. And there would be no point. There's nothing there. And if you want to get to civilisation that's a three-day walk through the rainforest—a rainforest with about twenty different kinds of venomous snakes living in it.'

'Does that include you?' she snarled.

But he had already closed the door.

Left alone, Nola pulled off her clothes and angrily yanked on her pyjamas. She still couldn't believe what was happening. How could he treat her like this?

Worse—how could he treat her like this and then expect her to sit down and have a civilised conversation with him?

She clenched her jaw. He could expect what he liked. But he couldn't make her talk or listen if she didn't want to.

Her eyes narrowed. In fact she might just stay in her room.

She would think about it properly in the morning. Right now she needed to close her eyes and, climbing into bed, she pulled the duvet up to her chin, rolled onto her side, and fell swiftly and deeply into sleep.

Ram strode into the huge open-plan living space, his frustration with Nola vying with his fury at himself.

What the hell was he doing?

He'd only just found out he was going to be a father. Surely that was enough to be dealing with right now? But apparently not, for he had decided to add to the chaos and drama of the evening by kidnapping Nola.

Because, regardless of what he had said to her in the car, this *was* kidnapping.

Groaning, he ran a hand wearily over his face.

But what choice had she given him?

Ever since she'd forced him to meet her at that internet café she had challenged him at every turn. But she was pregnant with his child now, and her leaving the country was more than defiance. Even though she'd said she would be in touch, he hadn't believed her.

His face hardened. And why should he? She had kept the pregnancy secret for months, and even when she'd had the perfect opportunity to tell him about the baby she had chosen instead to avoid him. And then tried to run away.

But Nola was going nowhere now. She certainly wasn't going to Scotland any time soon.

He breathed out slowly. In fact, make that *never*.

If she moved back to Edinburgh, then he would be cut out of his baby's life. Not only that, his child would grow up with another man as his father—with another man's name instead of his. Worse, he or she would grow up believing themselves to be a burden not worth bearing, a mistake to be regretted.

He would do whatever it took to stop that from happening.

Crossing the room, he poured himself a whisky and downed it in one mouthful.

Even kidnapping.

His chest tightened.

What had he been thinking?

But that was just it. He hadn't been thinking at all—he'd just reacted on impulse, his emotions blindly driving his actions, so that now he had a woman he barely knew, who was carrying a child he hadn't planned, sleeping in the spare room in what was supposed to be his private sanctuary from the world.

Gritting his teeth, he poured himself another whisky and drank that too.

So why had he brought Nola here?

But he knew why. He hadn't been exaggerating when he'd said that the house was secluded. It was luxurious, of course, but it was completely inaccessible to anyone without a small plane or helicopter, and on most days communicating with the outside world was almost impossible.

Here, he and Nola would be completely alone and they would be able to talk.

His fingers twitched against the empty glass.

Except that talking was the last thing he wanted to do with her. Particularly now that they were alone, miles from civilisation.

A pulse began to beat in his groin.

For a moment he stared longingly at the bottle

of whisky. But where Nola was concerned it would take a lot more than alcohol to lock down his libido. A cold shower might be better—and if that didn't work he might have to go and swim a few lengths in the pool. And then maybe a few more.

He'd do whatever was necessary to re-engage his brain so that tomorrow he could tell Nola exactly how this was all going to play out.

As soon as she woke Nola reached over to pick up her phone, holding her breath as she quickly punched in Anna's number. When that failed to connect she called the office, then Anna again, and then, just to be certain, her favourite takeaway pizzeria by the harbour. But each time she got the same recorded message, telling her that there was no network coverage, and finally she gave up.

Rolling onto her side, she gazed in silence around the bedroom. It was still dark, but unless she'd slept the entire day it must be morning. She wasn't planning on going anywhere, but there was no point in lying there in the dark. Sighing, she sat up. Immediately she heard a small click, and then daylight began filling the room as two huge blinds slid smoothly up into the ceiling.

She gasped. But it wasn't the daylight or the blinds or even the room itself that made her hold her breath. It was the pure, brilliant blue sky outside the window.

Heart pounding, she scrambled across the bed and gazed down at a huge canopy of trees, her eyes widening as a group of brightly coloured birds burst out of the dark green leaves. She watched open-mouthed as they circled one another, looping and curling in front of her window like miniature acrobatic planes, before suddenly plunging back into the trees.

She had been planning on staying in her room to protest against Ram's behaviour. But ten minutes later she had showered, dug some clean clothes out of her suitcase and was standing by her bedroom door.

Her pulse began to beat very fast. If she opened that door she would have to face Ram. But sooner or later she was going to have to face him anyway, she told herself firmly.

And, not giving herself the chance to change her mind, she stalked determinedly out of her room.

In daylight, the house was astonishingly, dazzlingly bright. Every wall was made of glass, and there were walkways at different levels, leading to platforms actually within the rainforest itself.

No doubt it had been designed that way, she thought slowly. So that the wildlife could be watched up close but safely in its natural environment.

Her heart began to thump.

Only some of the wildlife clearly didn't understand the rules, for there on the deck, standing at the edge of an infinity pool, was one of the most dangerous animals in Australia—probably in the world.

Unfortunately there was no safety glass between her and Ram.

She was on the verge of making a quick, unobtrusive retreat when suddenly he turned, and her breath seemed to slide sideways in her chest as he began slowly walking towards her.

It was the heat, she thought helplessly. Although she wasn't sure if it was the sun or the sight of Ram in swimming shorts that was making her skin feel warm and slick.

She tried not to stare, but he was so unbelievably gorgeous—all smooth skin and golden muscles. Now he was stopping in front of her and smiling, as though yesterday had never happened, and the stupid thing was that she didn't feel as though it had happened either. Or at least her body didn't.

'Good morning.' He squinted up at the sky. 'I think it still qualifies as morning.' Tilting his head, he let his eyes drift casually over her face. 'I was going to come and wake you up. But I didn't fancy getting punched on the nose.'

She met his gaze unwillingly. 'So you admit that I've got a reason to punch you, then?'

He grinned, and instantly she felt a tug low in her pelvis, heat splaying out inside her so quickly and fiercely that she thought she might pass out.

'I'm not sure if you need a reason,' he said softly. 'Most of the time I seem to annoy you just by existing.'

She gazed at him in silence, trying to remember why that was.

'Not always,' she said carefully. 'Only some of the time. Like when you kidnap me, for instance.'

There was a short, pulsing silence, and then finally he sighed.

'We need to talk about this now, Nola. Not in a week or a month. And, yes, maybe I overreacted, bringing you here like this. But you've been building a life, a future, that doesn't include me.'

Her heart gave a thump. 'I thought you *wanted* that.'

'What if I said I didn't?'

His eyes were fixed on her face.

She breathed out slowly, the world shifting out of focus around her.

'Then I guess we need to talk.'

'And we will.' His gaze locked onto hers. 'But first I'll give you the tour, and then you'd better eat something.'

The tour was brief, but mind-blowing. The house was minimalist in design—a stunning mix of metal and glass that perfectly offset the untamed beauty of the rainforest surrounding it.

Breakfast—or was it brunch?—took longer. A variety of cold meats, cheese, fruit and pastries were laid out buffet-style in the huge sunlit kitchen and, suddenly feeling famished, Nola helped herself to a plate of food and a cup of green tea while Ram watched with amusement.

'I have a live-in chef—Antoine. He's French, but he speaks very good English. If you have any particular likes or dislikes tell him. His wife, Sophie, is my housekeeper. She takes care of everything else. So if you need anything...'

Fingers tightening around her teacup, Nola met his gaze. 'Like what?'

He gave a casual shrug. 'I don't know. What about a bikini? You might fancy a swim.'

His eyes gleamed, and she felt something stir inside her as his gaze dropped over the plain white T-shirt that was just a fraction too small for her now.

'Unless, of course, you're planning on skinny-dipping.'

Ignoring the heat throbbing over her skin, she gave him an icy stare. 'I'm not planning on anything,' she said stiffly. 'Except leaving as soon as possible. I know we have a lot to talk about, but I hardly think it will take more than a day.'

He stared at her calmly. 'That will depend.'

'On what?'

He was watching her carefully, as though gauging her probable reaction to what he was about to say. But, really, given everything that he'd already said and done, how bad could it be?

'On what happens next. You see, I've given it a lot of thought,' he said slowly, 'and I can only think of one possible solution to this situation.'

Her nerves were starting to hum. She looked over at him impatiently. 'And? What is it?'

He stared at her for a long moment, and then finally he smiled.

'We need to marry. Preferably as soon as possible.'

CHAPTER SEVEN

NOLA STARED AT him in stunned silence.

Marry?

As her brain dazedly replayed his words inside her head she felt her skin grow hot, and then her heart began to bang against her ribs. Surely he couldn't be serious.

She laughed nervously. 'This is a joke, right?'

For a moment he looked at her in silence, then slowly he shook his head.

She stared at him incredulously. 'But you don't want to get married.' Her eyes widened with shock and confusion. 'Everyone knows that. You told me so yourself.' She frowned. 'You said marriage was a Mobius strip of emotional scenes.'

Watching the pulse beating frantically at the base of her throat, Ram felt a flicker of frustration.

To be fair, her reaction wasn't really surprising. He'd spent most of the night thinking along much the same lines himself. But, as he'd just told her, marriage was the only solution—the only way he could give his child the *right* kind of life. A life that was not just financially secure but filled with the kind of certainty that came from *belonging*.

He shrugged. 'I agree that it's not a choice I've

ever imagined making. But situations change, and I'm nothing if not adaptable.'

Adaptable! Nola felt her breathing jerk. What was he talking about? As soon as she'd shown the first signs of not wanting to do things his way he'd kidnapped her!

'Oh, I see—so that's what this is all about.' She loaded her voice with sarcasm. 'Dragging me out here, trying to coerce me into marrying you, is just your way of showing me how *adaptable* you are.' She gave a humourless laugh. 'You're about as adaptable as a tornado, Ram. If there's anything in your path it just gets swept away.'

'If that was true we wouldn't be having this conversation,' he said calmly.

'How is this a conversation?' Nola shook her head. 'You just told me we *need* to marry. That sounds more like an order than a proposal.'

His eyes narrowed. 'I'm sorry if you were hoping for something a little more romantic, but you didn't exactly give me much time to look for a ring.'

She glowered at him, anger buzzing beneath her skin. 'I don't want a ring. And I wasn't hoping for anything from you. In case you hadn't noticed, I've managed just fine without you for the last three months.'

His gaze didn't flicker.

'I wouldn't know,' he said softly. 'As you didn't

bother telling me you were having my baby until last night.'

Pushing away a twinge of guilt that she hadn't told him sooner, she gritted her teeth. It had been wrong of her not to tell him that she was pregnant. But marrying him wasn't going to put it right.

Only, glancing at the set expression on his face, she saw that Ram clearly thought it was.

Forcing herself to stay calm, she said quickly, 'And I've apologised. But why does that mean we need to get married?'

Ram felt his chest grow tight. Did he *really* need to answer that? His face hardened and he stared at her irritably. 'I would have thought that was obvious.'

For a fraction of a second his eyes held hers, and then he glanced pointedly down at her stomach.

'Because I'm *pregnant*?' She stared at him in exasperation, the air thumping out of her lungs. How could he do this? It was bad enough that he'd tricked her into coming here in the first place. But to sit there, so handsome and smug, making these absurd, arrogant statements... And then assume that she was just going to go along with them.

'Maybe a hundred years ago that might have been a reason. But it is possible to have a baby out of wedlock. People do it all the time now.'

'Not *my* baby,' Ram said flatly, his stomach clenching swiftly at her words.

How could she be so casual about this? So dismissive? Did she really think that having a father was discretionary? A matter of preference? Like having a dog or a cat?

He studied her face, seeing the fear and understanding it. *Good.* It was time she realised that he was being serious. Marriage wasn't an optional extra, like the adaptive suspension he'd had fitted on his latest Lamborghini. It was the endgame. The obvious denouement of that night on his sofa.

Shaking his head, trying to ignore the anger pooling there, he said coolly, 'By any definition this situation is a mess, and the simplest, most logical way to clear it up is for us to marry. Or are you planning on buying a crib and just hoping for the best?'

Nola felt her heartbeat trip over itself. How *dare* he?

She didn't know what was scaring her more. The fact that Ram was even considering this as an option, or his obvious belief that she was actually going to agree to it.

Looking up into his handsome face, she felt her skin begin to prickle. She couldn't agree. She might not have planned this pregnancy, but she knew she could make it work. Marrying Ram, though…

How could that be anything *but* a disaster?

They barely knew each other, had nothing in common, and managed to turn every single conversation into an argument. She swallowed. And, of course, they weren't in love—not even close to being in love.

Her head was spinning.

All they shared was this baby growing inside her, and one passionate night of sex. But marriages weren't built on one-night stands. And, no matter how incredible that night had been, she wasn't so naive as to believe that a man like Ram Walker would view his wedding vows as anything but guidelines.

Her fingers curved into the palms of her hands. For her—for most people—marriage meant commitment. Monogamy.

But Ram could barely manage five days with the same woman. So how exactly was he planning on forsaking all others?

Or was he expecting to be able to carry on just as he pleased?

Either way, how long would it be before he felt trapped...resentful?

Or, worse, bored?

Remembering the distracted look in her father's eyes, the sense that he was always itching to be somewhere else and her own panicky need to try and make him stay, she felt sick.

She knew instinctively that Ram would be the same.

Wanting Nola to be his wife was just the knee-jerk response of a CEO faced with an unexpected problem. But she didn't want her marriage to be an exercise in damage limitation. Surely he could understand that.

But, looking over at him, she felt a rush of panic.

He looked so calm, almost too calm, as though her opposition to his ludicrous suggestion was just a mere formality—some twisted version of bridal nerves.

And with any other woman he would probably be right in thinking that. After all, he'd almost certainly never met anyone who had turned him down.

Her heart began to pound.

Until now.

Slowly, she shook her head.

'I can't marry you, Ram. Right now, I'm not sure I ever want to be married. But if at some point I do, it will be because the man asking me *loves* me and wants me to be his wife.'

His face was expressionless, but his eyes were cool and resolute.

'And what happens if you don't marry? I doubt you'll stay single for ever, so how will that work? Are you going to live with a man? Is he just going to spend the occasional night in your bed?'

She felt her face drain of colour.

'I don't know. And you can't expect me to be

able to answer all those questions now. That's not
fair—'

His eyes were locked on hers.

'*I don't know* is not a good enough answer,' he
said coldly. 'And the life you're planning for our
child sounds anything but fair.'

'I'm not planning anything.' She stared at him
helplessly.

'Well, at least we can agree on that,' he snarled.
'Believe me, Nola, when I tell you that no child
of mine is going to be brought up by whichever
random man happens to be in your life at that particular moment.'

'That's not—' She started to protest but he cut
her off.

'Nor is my child going to end up with another
man's name because its mother was too stubborn
and selfish to marry its father.'

She stood up so quickly the chair she was sitting
on flew backwards. But neither of them noticed.

'Oh, I see. So you marrying me is a *selfless* act,'
she snapped. Her blue eyes flashed angrily up at
him. 'A real sacrifice—'

'You're putting words in my mouth.'

'And you're putting a gun to my head,' she re-
torted. 'I'm not going to marry you just to satisfy
your archaic need to pass on a name.'

'Names matter.'

She shivered. 'You mean *your* name matters.'

Ram felt his chest tighten. Yes, he did mean that. A name was more than just a title. It was an identity, a destiny, a piece of code from the past that mapped out the future.

His eyes locked onto hers. 'Children need to know where they come from. They need to belong.'

'Then what's wrong with *my* name?' she said stubbornly. 'I'm the mother. This baby is inside *me*. How could it belong to anyone more than to me?'

'Now you're just being contrary.'

'Why? Because I don't want to marry you?'

He shook his head, his dark gaze locked onto hers. 'Because you know I'm right but you're mad at me for bringing you here so you're just going to reject the only logical solution without a moment's consideration.'

Nola felt despair edge past her panic. His cavalier attitude to her objections combined with his obvious belief that she would crumble was overwhelming her.

'I have considered it and it won't work,' she said quickly. 'And it doesn't have to. Look, this is *my* responsibility. I should have been more careful. That's why this is on *me*.'

'This is *on you*?' He repeated her words slowly, his voice utterly expressionless.

But as she looked over at him she felt the hairs on the back of her neck stand up. His eyes were narrowed, fixed on her face like a sniper.

'We're not talking about a round of drinks, Nola. This is a baby. A life.'

She flinched. 'Biology is not a determining factor in parenthood.'

He looked at her in disbelief. 'Seriously? Did you read that in the in-flight magazine?'

She looked at him helplessly. 'No, I just meant—'

He cut her off again. 'Tell me, Nola. Did you have a father?'

The floor seemed to tilt beneath her feet. 'Yes. But I don't—'

'But you don't what?' He gave a short, bitter laugh. 'You don't want that for your own child?'

She blinked. Tears were pricking at her eyes. But she wasn't going to lose control—at least not here and now, in front of Ram.

'You're right,' she said shakily. 'I don't want that. And I never will.'

And before he had a chance to reply she turned and walked swiftly out of the kitchen.

She walked blindly, her legs moving automatically in time to the thumping of her heart, wanting nothing more than to find somewhere to hide, somewhere dark and private, away from Ram's cold, critical gaze. Somewhere she could curl up and cradle the cold ache of misery inside her.

Her feet stopped. Somehow she had managed to find the perfect place—a window looking out into the canopy of the rainforest. There was even a sofa and, her legs trembling, she sat down, her throat burning, hands clenched in her lap.

For a moment she just gazed miserably into the trees, and then abruptly her whole body stilled as she noticed a pair of eyes gazing back at her. Slowly, she inched forward—and just like that they were gone.

'It was a goanna. If you sit here long enough it will probably come back.'

She turned as Ram sat down next to her on the sofa.

She stared at him warily, shocked not only by the fact that he had come to find her but by the fact that his anger, the hardness in his eyes, had faded.

'Did I scare it?'

Ram held her gaze. 'They're just cautious— they run away when something or someone gets too close.'

Watching her lip tremble, he felt his heart start to pound. She looked so stricken...so small.

His breath caught in his throat. In his experience women exploited emotion with the skill and precision of a samurai wielding a sword. But Nola was different. She hadn't wanted him to see that she was upset. On the contrary, she had been as desperate to get away as that lizard.

Desperate to get away from *him*.

An ache was spreading inside his chest and he gritted his teeth, not liking the way it made him feel, for he would never hurt her. In fact he had wanted more than anything to reach out and pull her against him. But of course he hadn't. Instead he'd watched her leave.

Only almost immediately, and for the first time in his life, he'd been compelled to follow. He'd had no choice—his legs had been beyond his conscious control.

He stared at her in silence, all at once seeing not only the tight set of her shoulders and the glint of tears but also what he'd chosen to ignore earlier: her vulnerability.

Shifting back slightly, to give her more space, he cleared his throat.

'There's always something to see,' he said carefully. 'We could stay and watch if you want?'

He phrased it as a question—something he would never normally do. But right now getting her to relax, to trust him, seemed more important than laying down the law.

She didn't reply, and he felt an unfamiliar twitch of panic that maybe she never would.

But finally she nodded. 'I'd like that. Apart from the odd squirrel, I've never seen anything wild up close.'

'Too busy studying?'

It was a guess, but she nodded again.

'I did work too hard,' she agreed. 'I think it was a survival technique.'

Staring past him, Nola bit her lip. She'd spoken without thinking, the words coming from deep inside. Memories came of hours spent hunched over her schoolbooks, trying to block out the raised voices downstairs, and then—worse—the horrible, bleak silence that had always followed.

Ram stared at her uncertainly, hating the bruised sound of her voice. This was the sort of conversation he'd spent a lifetime avoiding. Only this time he didn't want to avoid it. In fact he was actually scared of spooking her, and suddenly he was desperate to say something—anything to make her trust him enough to keep talking.

'Why do you think that?' he asked gently.

She swallowed. 'My dad was often home late, or away, and my parents would always argue when he got home. He'd storm off, and my mum would cry, and I'd stay in my room and do my homework.'

The ache in her voice cut him almost as much as her words, for he was beginning to understand now why she was so determined to stay single, so vehemently opposed even to letting him know about the baby.

'Are they still together?'

She shook her head.

'They divorced when I was seven. At first it was better. It was calmer at home, and my dad made a real effort. He even promised to take me to the zoo in Edinburgh for my birthday. Only he forgot. Not just about the zoo, but about my birthday too.'

Ram felt as though he'd been punched hard in the face. He felt a vicious, almost violent urge to find her father and tell him exactly what he thought of him.

She breathed out unsteadily. 'About two months later I got a card and some money. The following year he forgot my birthday again. One year he even managed to forget me at Christmas. Of course when he remembered I got the biggest, glitziest present…'

Nola could feel Ram's gaze on her face, but she couldn't look at him. She couldn't let him see what her father had seen and rejected: her need to be loved. Couldn't bear for him to guess her most closely guarded secret. That she hadn't been enough of a reason for her father to make the effort.

'I thought he'd stopped loving my mum, and that was why he left. But he didn't love me either, and he left me too.'

'And that's what you think I'd do?'

Turning her head, she finally met his eyes. 'You have to put children first. Only sometimes people just can't do that, and I'm not blaming them…'

His grey eyes were searching her face, and she felt a rush of panic. How could she expect Ram to understand? He wouldn't know what it was like to feel so unimportant, so easy to forget, so disposable.

'Sometimes you have to give people a chance too,' he said quietly.

Nola bit her lip. His voice sounded softer, and she could sense that he was if not backing down then backing off, trying to calm her. But her heart was still beating too fast for her to relax. And anyway... Her pulse shivered violently... It wasn't as though he was going to change his mind. He was just trying a different tactic, biding his time while he waited for her to give in.

Suddenly she could no longer rein in the panic rising up inside her. 'I can't do this, Ram. I know you think I'm just being difficult. But I'm not. I know what marrying the wrong person can do people. It's just so damaging and destructive. And what's worse is that even when the marriage ends that damage doesn't stop. It just goes on and on—'

'Nola.'

Her body tensed as he lifted a hand and stroked a long dark curl away from her face.

'I'm not going to behave like your father did. I'm not walking away from you, or our baby. I'm fighting to make it work. Why do you think I want to marry you?'

She shook her head. 'You want it *now*. But soon you'll start to think differently, and then you'll *feel* differently. And we hardly know each other,

Ram. Having a baby won't change that, and there is nothing else between us.'

His gaze seemed to burn into hers. 'We both know that's not true.'

She swallowed. 'That was one night…'

'Was it?' Ram studied her face. He could see the conflict in her eyes, and with shock he realised that it mirrored what he was feeling himself—the longing, the fear, the confusion. The pain.

He didn't want to feel her pain, or his own. He didn't want to feel anything. And for a fraction of a second he was on the verge of pulling her into his arms and doing what he always did to deflect emotion—his own and other people's.

But something held him back—a sudden understanding that if he didn't allow himself to feel, then he would never be able to comfort Nola, and right now that was all that mattered.

Not himself, nor his business, the launch, or even getting her to agree to this marriage, but Nola herself.

In shock, clenching his hands until they hurt, he gazed past her, struggling to explain this wholly uncharacteristic behaviour.

Surely, though, it was only natural for him to care. Nola was carrying his child.

Turning, he breathed out slowly, staring down into her eyes. 'I know you don't trust me. And if I were you I'd feel exactly the same. I haven't exactly given you much reason to have faith in me, bringing you here like I have.'

He grimaced.

'I just wanted to give us some time and some privacy. I didn't think we could sort things out with everything else going on, and I still think that. But I'm not going to force you to marry me, Nola. Or even to stay here if you don't want to.'

Reaching into his pocket, he pulled out a phone and held it out to her, watching her eyes widen with confusion.

'I didn't lie to you. There is no coverage here. That's why I have this. It's a satellite phone. If you want to leave you can call the pilot. If you stay, I want it to be your choice.'

Nola stared at him, her tears beaten back by Ram's words. This was a concession. More than that, it was a chance to get her life back.

She glanced down at the phone, her brain fast-forwarding. They could handle this through their lawyers. There was probably no need even to see one another again. But was that really what she wanted? What was best for their baby?

'I'll stay.' She held his gaze. 'But I might ring Anna later, or tomorrow. Just to let her know I'm okay.'

He pocketed the phone and nodded, and then after the briefest hesitation he reached over and took her hand in his.

'I know this is a big step for both of us, Nola. But I think we can make it work if we compromise a little.'

Nola gazed at him blankly. 'Compromise?'

He frowned. 'That *is* a word, isn't it?'

She smiled weakly. 'It is. I'm just not sure you understand what it means. Maybe you're thinking of another word.'

His grey eyes softened, and she felt her pulse dip as he lifted her hand to his mouth and kissed it gently. 'Let's see…I think it means I have to stop acting like a tornado and listen to what you're saying.'

She felt her stomach drop. Ram might have been difficult to defy when he was angry, but he was impossible to resist when he was smiling.

'That sounds like a compromise,' she said cautiously. 'But what does it mean in real terms?'

'It means that I think we need time to get used to the idea of getting married and to each other.'

She bit her lip. 'How much time?'

'As long as it takes.' He met her gaze. 'I'll wait, Nola. For as long as it takes.'

Her pulse was jumping again. For a moment they stared at one another, breathing unsteadily, and then finally she gave him a hesitant smile.

'That could work.'

And maybe it would, for suddenly she knew that for the first time she was actually willing to consider marrying him.

* * *

They spent the rest of the morning together, watching lizards and frogs and birds through the glass. Ram knew a surprising amount about the various animals and plants, and she found herself not only relaxing, but enjoying herself and his company.

So much so that as she dialled Anna's number the following morning she found it increasingly difficult to remember that he was the same person who had made her feel so horribly trapped and desperate.

'So let me get this right,' Anna said slowly down the phone. 'You're staying with Ram Walker in his rainforest treehouse. Just you and him. Even though we don't work for him anymore. And you think that's normal?'

'I didn't say that,' Nola protested, glancing over to where Ram lay lounging in the sun, a discarded paperback on the table beside him. 'Obviously nothing he does is normal. He's the richest man in Australia. I just said that me being here is not that big a deal.'

Her friend gave a short, disbelieving laugh. 'Is that why I wasn't invited?'

Nola grimaced. 'You weren't invited because you're in Edinburgh. With a broken foot and a husband.'

'I *knew* it!' Anna said triumphantly. 'So there *is* something going on!'

'No!' Nola froze as Ram turned and glanced over at her curiously. Lowering her voice, she said quickly. 'Well, it's complicated...'

She badly wanted to tell her best friend the truth. Sooner or later she would have to. Her fingers gripped the phone more tightly.

'I'm pregnant, and Ram's the father.'

Her words hung in silence down the phone and she closed her eyes, equal parts of hope and fear rising up inside her. What if Anna was disgusted? Or never wanted to speak to her again?

'That's why I'm here. We're talking things through.' Breathing out shakily, she pressed the phone against her face. 'I wanted to tell you before, but—'

'It was complicated?'

Nola opened her eyes with relief. Her friend's voice was gentle, and full of love. It was going to be okay.

'I'm sorry. I just couldn't get think straight.'

Anna laughed. 'That's okay. I forgive you as long as you tell me everything now.'

She didn't tell Anna everything, but she gave her friend an edited version of the last few days. But even while she was talking she was thinking about Ram. Having finally stopped fighting him, all she wanted was to concentrate on the two of them building a relationship that would work for their child.

That was, after all, the reason she'd decided to stay.

The only reason.

Her cheeks grew hotter.

Try telling that to her body.

Her mouth was suddenly dry. Staring across the deck at Ram, she felt her breath catch fire. It was true, she *did* want a relationship with him that would work for their child. But that didn't mean she could deny the way her body reacted to his. Even now, just looking at him was playing havoc with her senses. And up close he seemed to trigger some internal alarm system, so that she felt constantly restless, her body shivering and tightening and melting all at the same time.

But her relationship with Ram was already complicated enough. So it didn't matter that no man had ever made her feel the way he had. Giving in to the sexual pull between them would only add another layer of complication neither of them needed.

Her mouth twisted.

Maybe if she told herself that often enough, she might actually start to believe it.

'So,' Ram said softly, as she sat down beside him and handed him the phone, 'is everything okay?'

She nodded. 'Yes. I told her about the baby. She was a little…' she hesitated, searching for the right word '…stunned at first, but she was cool about it.'

Ram studied her face. Since agreeing to stay, Nola had seemed more relaxed, but he couldn't shift the image from his head of her looking so small and crushed, and impulsively he reached out and ran his fingers over her arm.

'You need to be careful. Are you wearing enough sunblock?'

She grimaced. 'Loads. I used to try and tan, but it never works. I just burn and then peel, so now I am fully committed to factor fifty.'

'Is that right?' His gaze roamed over her face. 'Then I'm jealous. I only want you to be fully committed to *me*.'

Nola blinked. He must be teasing her, she decided. Ram might want to marry her in order to legitimise this pregnancy, but he didn't do commitment. And jealousy would require an emotional response she knew he wasn't capable of or willing to give. But knowing that didn't stop her stomach flipping over in response to the possessiveness in his words.

Hoping her thought process wasn't showing on her face, she said lightly, 'You've got bigger competition than a bottle of sunblock.'

His eyes narrowed. 'I do?'

He let his fingers curl around her wrist, and then gently he pulled her towards him so that suddenly their eyes were level.

'I thought you said you didn't have anyone missing you,' he said softly.

She bit her lip. 'I don't think he does miss me. He's quite self-sufficient...' Glancing up at the stubble shadowing his jaw, she smiled. 'A little prickly. A bit like you, really. Except he's green, and he's got this cute little pot like a sombrero.'

Ram shook his head. 'I can't believe you're comparing me to a cactus.'

She laughed. 'There's no comparison. Colin is a low-maintenance dream. Whereas you—'

His eyes were light and dancing with amusement. 'I'm what?'

She felt her pulse begin to flutter. 'You have a private jet and a house in the rainforest.'

'And you care about that?'

She glanced up. Something in his tone had shifted, and he was watching her, his grey gaze oddly intent.

'No, I don't,' she said truthfully. It might sound rude, or ungrateful but she wasn't going to lie just to flatter him. 'It's lovely to have all this, but it doesn't matter to me. Other things are more important.'

Her father had taught her that. His gifts had always been over the top—embarrassingly so in comparison to what her mother had chosen for her. But there had been no thought involved, nothing personal about his choice. Nothing personal about the money he'd sent either, except that it had grown exponentially in relation to his neglect.

'Like what?

Ram was gazing at her curiously, but just as she opened her mouth to reply, his phone rang.

Glancing down at it, he frowned. 'Excuse me. I have to take this.'

Standing up, he walked away, his face tight with concentration.

She caught bits of the conversation, but nothing that gave her any clue as to who the caller might be. Not that she needed any. It would be work-related, because of course, despite what he'd said and what she'd chosen to believe, work would always come first. She just hadn't expected to have it pointed out to her quite so quickly.

Finally he hung up.

'Sorry about that.' His face was impassive, but there was a tension in his voice that hadn't been there before.

Looking up, she forced herself to smile casually, even though she felt flattened inside. 'When do they want you back?'

'Who?' He stared at her blankly.

'Work. Do you need to leave now?'

Ram didn't answer. He was too busy processing the realisation that since getting off the plane he hadn't thought about work once. Even the launch seemed to belong to another life he had once lived. And forgotten.

He shook his head.

'It wasn't work. It was Pandora. My mother. I was supposed to have lunch with my parents today, only with everything that's happened I forgot.'

Catching sight of Nola's face, he shrugged.

'It's fine—honestly. My mother's portions are so tiny it's hardly worth the effort of going, and besides it gives Guy, my father, a chance to complain about me, so—'

'You could still go,' she said hastily. 'I can just stay here and—'

She stopped mid-sentence as his eyes locked onto hers.

'Why would you stay here?

'I don't know.' She hesitated. 'I just thought… I mean, obviously I'd like to meet them.'

Was that true? Her pulse jumped.

She was still wary of escalating their relationship too fast. But was that because her perception of marriage was so skewed by the past? Maybe lunch with Ram's family would help balance out her point of view. And, more importantly, it might give her some insight into the father of her child, for while she had talked a lot—about herself, her parents, even her cactus—Ram was still a mystery to her.

Take his parents. She didn't know anything about them. If she'd been shaped by her mother and father, then surely it was logical to assume that Ram had been shaped by his parents too. So why not take this opportunity to see what they were like? For the sake of their child, of course.

She glanced up at him hesitantly. 'Would you like me to meet them?'

Ram stared at her in silence, wondering how best to answer that question. Nola meeting his parents had not been part of the equation when he'd brought her here. Yet clearly she was trying to meet him halfway, and as it had been he who had suggested they get to know one another better it seemed churlish to refuse.

But going to lunch with them would mean leaving the rainforest, and he didn't want to do that.

He wanted to stay here with Nola. For it to be just the two of them. There was no need to involve Pandora and Guy. Only how could he explain that without having to explain who he was and *what* he was…?

His chest tightened.

Lifting his face, he smiled coolly. 'Of course. It will give me a chance to drop in at the office. There are a couple of papers I need. I'll ring her back and see if she can do tomorrow.'

CHAPTER EIGHT

THEY FLEW BACK to Sydney the next day.

Gazing out of the window, Nola wished her thoughts were as calm as the clear blue sky beyond the glass. It was hard to believe that only a few days ago she'd fled from the RWI building. So much had happened since then. So much had changed. Not least her perception of Ram.

She had believed him to be domineering, insensitive and unemotional, but as she glanced across the aircraft to where he stood, joking with the cabin crew, she knew that he was a different man than she'd thought.

Yes, he had as good as abducted her from the airport but, seeing her upset, he had backed down, given her the option of leaving. And he'd been unexpectedly gentle and understanding when she'd told him about her father.

Shifting in her seat, she bit her lip. She still didn't really understand why she had confided in Ram. The words had just spilled out before she'd been able to stop them. But she didn't regret it, for they had both learnt something about one another as a result.

Yet now she was about to meet *his* parents, and she could feel all her old nervousness creeping over her skin. Glancing down at her skirt, she pressed her hands against the fabric, smoothing out an imaginary crease.

If only they could just stay here on the plane, circling the earth for ever...

She jumped slightly as Ram sat down beside her, and plucked her hand from her lap. Threading his fingers through hers, he rested his grey eyes on her face.

'So, what's bothering you, then?'

'Nothing,' she protested.

'You haven't said more than two words since we got on the plane. And you're fidgeting. So let's start with the obvious first. What have I done?'

She shook her head again. 'You haven't done anything.'

'Okay. What have I said? Or not said?'

Despite her nerves, she couldn't help smiling.

'It's not you...it's nothing—' She stopped, suddenly at a loss for words. 'It's just been such a long time since I've done a family lunch, and spending time with my mum and dad was always so stressful.'

'Then you don't need to worry,' he said dryly. 'My parents are the perfect hosts. They would never do anything to make a guest feel uncomfortable.'

She frowned. There was an edge to his voice that hadn't been there before.

'Are you sure they don't mind me coming along too? I don't want to put them to any trouble.'

He smiled—an odd, twisted smile that made her heart lurch forward.

'Pandora is the queen of the charity dinner and the benefit dance. She loves entertaining, and Guy does as he's told, so you coming to lunch will be absolutely no trouble at all.'

Her heart felt as if it were high up in her chest.

'And who do they think I am? I mean, in relation to you?' She hesitated. 'Have you told them about the baby?'

His face was expressionless. 'No. They don't need to know. As to who you are—I told them you used to work for me, and that now we're seeing one another.'

As she opened her mouth to protest, he shrugged.

'You're the first woman I've ever taken to meet them.' His grey eyes watched her steadily, his mouth tugging up at the corners. 'It was either that or pretend you were coming to fix the hard drive.'

They landed in Sydney an hour later. Ram's limo was waiting for them at the edge of the private airfield, and soon they were cruising along the motorway.

But instead of turning towards the city centre, as she'd expected, the car carried on.

'Didn't you want to go to the office first?' Frowning, Nola glanced over to where Ram was gazing down at his phone.

'I changed my mind.' He looked up, his face impassive. 'I thought you might like to freshen up, and I need to pick up a car.'

'Where are we going?'

He smiled. 'We're going home.'

She frowned. 'I thought you had a penthouse in the city?'

He shrugged. 'I do. It's convenient for work. But it's not my home.'

Home.

The word made her think of her flat in Edinburgh, her shabby sofas and mismatched crockery. But home for Ram turned out to be something altogether grander—a beautiful white mansion at the end of a private drive.

Stepping dazedly out of the car, Nola felt her heart jump. She'd recognised the name of the road as soon as they'd started to drive down it. How could she not? It was regularly cited as being the most expensive place to live in the country, and Ram's house more than lived up to that reputation.

'Welcome to Stanmore.' He was standing beside her, smiling, watching her face casually, but she could sense a tension beneath his smile, and suddenly she knew that he cared what she thought— and that fact made her throat tighten so that she couldn't speak.

'It's incredible,' she managed finally.

A couple of hours ago she'd denied being intimidated by his wealth, but now she wasn't sure that was still true. For a moment she hesitated, caught between fear and curiosity, but then his hand caught hers and he tugged her forward.

'I'm glad you think so. Now, come on. I want to show you round.'

As they wandered through the beautiful interior Nola caught her breath, her body transformed into a churning mass of insecurity. How could Ram seriously expect them to marry? This was a different world from hers. And no doubt his parents would realise that the moment she walked through their door.

'My great-great-grandfather, Stanley Armitage, bought this land in 1864,' Ram said casually as he led her into a beautiful living room with uninterrupted views of the ocean. 'I'm the fifth generation of my family to live here.'

Nola nodded. 'So you grew up here?'

His face didn't change but his eyes narrowed slightly.

'My mother moved out when she got married. They live just along the road. But I spent most of my holidays here, aside from the odd duty dinner with my parents.' He paused. 'Which reminds me... We should probably think about getting ready.'

Nola gazed down at her skirt and blouse in dismay. They had looked fine when she'd put them on that morning, but after two hours of travelling she felt sticky and dishevelled.

'I can't meet your parents looking like this.'

'So don't,' he said easily.

'But I don't have anything else.'

'Yes, you do.'

Before she had a chance to reply, he was towing her upstairs, through one of the bedrooms and into a large dressing room.

'I know you acted cool about it, but I thought you might worry about being underdressed, so I spoke to my mother's stylist and she sent these over this morning.'

Hanging from a rail were at least twenty outfits in clear, protective wrappers.

Nola gazed at them speechlessly.

He grinned, obviously pleased by her reaction. 'Pick something you like. I think there are shoes as well. I'm just going to go change.'

She nodded. But picking something was not as easy as Ram's throwaway remark had implied. The clothes were all so beautiful… Finally she settled on a pale blue dress with a pretty ribbon-edged cardigan that cleverly concealed her bump. Her cheeks were already flushed, so she didn't bother with any blusher, but she brushed her hair until it lay smoothly over her shoulders, and then added a smudge of clear lip gloss.

'You look beautiful.'

Turning, she caught her breath. Ram was lounging in the doorway, his grey eyes glittering with approval.

'So do you,' she said huskily, her gaze drifting over his dark suit and cornflower-blue shirt.

Holding out his hand, he grinned. 'Who? Me? I'm just here to drive the car.'

The car turned out to be a Lamborghini, low to the ground and an eye-catching bright blue.

As they drove the short distance to his parents' house she couldn't resist teasing him about the colour. 'Did you choose the car to match your shirt?'

He gave her a heartbreaking smile. 'No, your eyes,' he said softly. 'Now, stop distracting me.'

She bit her lip, her expression innocent. 'I distract you?'

Shaking his head, he grimaced. 'More like bewitch me. Since I met you in that café I haven't been able to concentrate on anything. I've hardly done any work for months. If I wasn't me, I'd fire myself.'

Glancing out of the window, with his words humming inside her head, she felt suddenly ridiculously happy—even though, she reminded herself quickly, Ram was really only talking about the sexual chemistry between them.

Two minutes later he shifted down a gear and turned into a driveway. Nola could see tennis courts and a rectangle of flawless green grass.

'It's a putting green,' Ram said quietly. 'Guy is a big golf fan.'

She nodded. Of course it was a putting green.

But then the putting green was forgotten, for suddenly she realised why Ram had taken her to his house first.

As he switched off the engine she breathed out slowly. 'You thought all this would scare me, didn't you? That's why we went to Stanmore first.'

He shrugged, but the intensity of his gaze told her that she was right.

Reaching out, she touched his hand tentatively. 'Thank you.'

He caught her fingers in his, his eyes gently mocking her. 'I was a little concerned at how you might react. But, as you can see, I'm way richer than they are...'

She punched him lightly on the arm.

'I can't believe you said that.'

Leaning forward, he tipped her face up to his. 'Can't you?' he said softly. 'Then your opinion of me must be improving.'

For a moment time seemed to slow, and they

gazed at one another in silence until finally she cleared her throat.

'Do you think we should go in?'

'Of course.' He let go of her chin. 'Let's go and eat.'

Walking swiftly through the house, Ram felt as though his chest might burst. He couldn't quite believe that he'd brought Nola here. One way or another it was asking for trouble—especially as his relationship with her was still at such a delicate stage. But avoiding his parents wasn't an option either—not if he was serious about getting Nola to trust him.

Aware suddenly that she was struggling to keep up with him, he slowed his pace and gave her an apologetic smile. 'Sorry. I think they must be in the garden room.'

The garden room! Was that some kind of conservatory? Nola wondered as she followed Ram's broad back.

Yes, it was, she concluded a moment later as she walked into a light, exquisitely furnished room. But only in the same way that Ram's rainforest hideaway was some kind of treehouse.

'Finally! I was just about to ring you, Ramsay.'

Pulse racing, Nola swung round. The voice was high and clear, and surprisingly English-sounding. But not as surprising as the woman who was sashaying towards them.

Ram smiled coolly. 'Hello, Mother.'

Nola gazed speechlessly at Pandora Walker. Tall, beautiful and blonde, wearing an expensive silk dress that showed off her slim arms and waist, she looked more like a model than a mother—certainly not one old enough to have a son Ram's age.

'You said one o'clock, and it's two minutes past,' Ram said without any hint of apology, leaning forward to kiss her on both cheeks.

'Five by my watch.' She gave him an indulgent smile. 'I'm not fussing on my account, darling, it's just that you know your father hates to be kept waiting.

Glancing past them, she pursed her lips.

'Not that he has any qualms about keeping everyone else hanging around. Or ruining the food.'

Nola stilled. Goosebumps were covering her arms. For a fraction of second it could have been her own mother speaking.

But that thought was quickly forgotten as, shaking his head, Ram turned towards Nola and said quietly, 'The food will be perfect. It always is. Nola, this is my mother, Pandora. Mother, this is Nola Mason. She's one of the consultants I hired to work on the launch.'

Smiling politely, Nola felt a jolt of recognition as she met Pandora's eyes—for they were the exact same colour and shape as Ram's. But where had he got that beautiful black hair?

'Thank you so much for inviting me,' she said quickly. 'It's really very kind of you.'

Pandora leaned forward and brushed her cheek lightly against Nola's.

'No, thank *you* for coming. I can't tell you how delightful it is to meet you. Ram is usually so secretive. If I want to know anything at all about his private life I have to read about it in the papers. Ah, finally, here's Guy. Darling, we've all been waiting...'

Nola felt another shiver run over her skin. Pandora was still smiling, but there was an edge of coolness to her voice as a tall, handsome man with blond hair and light brown eyes strolled into the room.

'Ramsay, your mother and I were so sure you'd forget I booked to have lunch with Ted Shaw at the club. Just had to ring and cancel.' He turned towards Nola. 'Guy Walker—and you must be Nola.'

'It's lovely to meet you, Mr Walker.'

He smiled—a long, curling smile that reached his eyes.

'Call me Guy, please, and the pleasure is all mine.'

Ram might get his grey eyes from his mother, Nola thought as she followed Pandora out of the room to lunch, but he'd clearly inherited his charm from his father.

To her relief, she quickly discovered that Ram had been telling the truth about his parents. They were the perfect hosts: beautiful, charming and entertaining. And the food was both delicious and exquisitely presented. And yet somehow she couldn't shift the feeling that there was an undercurrent of tension weaving unseen beneath the charm and the smooth flow of conversation.

'So what is it you did, then, Nola? For RWI, I mean?' Leaning forward, Guy poured himself another glass of wine.

'I'm a cyber architect. I designed and installed the new security system.'

He frowned. 'That's a thing now, is it?'

Nola opened her mouth, but before she could reply Ram said quietly, 'It's been a "thing" for a long time now. All businesses have cyber security teams. They have to. Big, global companies like RWI even more so. They're a prime target for hackers, and if we get hacked we lose money.'

Guy lifted his glass. 'By *we* you mean *you*.' He smiled conspiratorially at Nola. 'I might have given him my name but it's not a family business.'

She blinked. Taken at face value, Guy's comment was innocuous enough: a simple, statement of fact about who owned RWI. So why did his words feel like a shark's fin cutting through the surface of a swimming pool?

'Actually, I think what Ram is trying to say is that hacking is like any other kind of theft,' she said hurriedly. 'Like shoplifting or insurance fraud. In the end the costs get passed on to the consumers so everyone loses out.'

Feeling Ram's gaze on the side of her face, she turned and gave him a quick, tight smile. He nodded, not smiling exactly, but his eyes softened so that for a fraction of a second she almost felt as if they were alone.

Watching the faint flush of colour creep over Nola's cheeks, Ram felt his throat tighten.

He couldn't help but admire her. She was nervous—he could hear it in her voice. But she had defended him, and the fact that she cared enough to do that made his head spin, for nobody had *ever* taken his side. He'd learnt early in life to rely on no one but himself. Some days it felt as though his whole life had been one long, lonely battle.

Not that he'd cared.

Until now.

Until Nola.

But spending time with her over the last few days had been a revelation. Having never cohabited before, he'd expected to find it difficult—boring, even. But he'd enjoyed her company. She was beautiful, smart, funny, and she challenged him. And now she had gone into battle for him, so that the solitude and independence he had once valued so highly seemed suddenly less important. Unnecessary, unwelcome even.

'I'll have to take your word for it.' Guy laughed. 'Like I said, I might be a Walker but I'm not a hot-shot businessman like my son.'

Draining his glass, he leaned forward towards Nola.

'A long time ago I used to be an actor—quite a good one, actually. Right now, though, I'm just a party planner!'

Nola stared at him confusedly. 'You plan parties?'

'Ignore him, Nola, he's just being silly.' Pandora frowned at her husband, her lips tightening. 'We're having a party for our thirtieth wedding anniversary, and Guy's been helping with some of the arrangements.'

'Thirty years!' Nola smiled. 'That's wonderful.'

And it was. Only as Ram reached out and adjusted his water glass she felt her smile stiffen, for how did that make him feel? Hearing her sound so enthusiastic about his parents' thirtieth wedding anniversary when she'd been so fiercely against marrying him.

But then Ram only wanted to marry her because he felt he should, she thought defensively. His parents, on the other hand, had clearly loved each other from the start, and they were still in love now, thirty years later.

'Oh, you're so sweet.' Pandora gave her a pouting pink smile. "It's going to be a wonderful evening, but there's still so much to sort out. Only apparently *my* input is not required.'

So that was why she and Guy were so on edge.

Glancing over to see Guy was pouring himself another glass of wine, Nola felt a rush of relief at having finally found an explanation for the tensions around the table.

Guy scowled. 'You're right—it's not.' He picked up his glass. 'Doesn't stop you giving it, though. Which is one of the reasons why there's still so much to sort out.'

For perhaps a fraction of a second Pandora's beautiful face hardened, and then almost immediately she was smiling again.

'I know, darling. But at least we have one less thing to worry about now.' As Guy gazed at her blankly, she shook her head. 'Ram's guest. You *are* bringing Nola to the party, aren't you, Ramsay?'

There was a tiny suspended silence.

Nola froze. That aspect of the party hadn't even occurred to her. But obviously Ram would be going. Her heartbeat resonated in her throat as he turned towards her.

'Of course.'

Breath pummelled her lungs as he held her

gaze, his cool, grey eyes silencing her confusion and shock.

'She's looking forward to it—aren't you, sweetheart?'

She gazed at him in silence, too stunned to reply. Over the last few days she had spent some of the most intense and demanding hours of her life with Ram. She had revealed more to him about herself than to any other person, and she had seen a side to him that few people knew existed.

But his parents' party was going to be big news, and although it was unlikely anyone would be interested in her on her own, as one half of a couple with Ram...

Her pulse fluttered.

She knew enough about his private life to know that it wasn't private at all, and that as soon she stepped out in public with him there would be a feeding frenzy—and that wasn't what she wanted at all.

Or was it?

Suddenly she was fighting her own heartbeat. Definitely she didn't want the feeding frenzy part, but she would be lying if she said that she didn't want the chance to walk into a room on his arm. And not just because he was so heart-stoppingly handsome and sexy.

She liked him.

A lot.

And the more she got to know him the more she liked him.

Looking up, she met his gaze, and nodded slowly. 'Yes, I'm really excited.'

Pandora clapped her hands together. 'Wonderful,' she purred. 'In that case I must give you the number of my stylist...'

After lunch, they returned to Stanmore.

Ram worked while Nola sat watching the boats in the harbour. After a light supper he excused himself, claiming work again, and she went upstairs to shower and get ready for bed.

Standing beneath the warm water, she closed her eyes and let her mind drift.

The drive home had been quiet—supper too. But then both of them had a lot to think about. Introducing her to his parents had probably been about as a big deal for Ram as meeting them had been for her.

Turning off the shower, she wrapped a towel around herself. And then, of course, there was the party. Her heart began to thump loudly inside her chest. Was that why he'd been so quiet? Was he regretting letting himself be chivvied into taking her as his guest?

But as she walked back into the bedroom that question went unanswered, for there, sitting on her bed, was Ram.

She stopped, eyes widening with surprise. 'I thought you were going to do some work?'

Glancing past her, he shrugged. 'I was worried about you. You seemed...' He hesitated, frowning. 'Distracted.'

There was an edge to his voice that she couldn't quite pinpoint.

'I'm just tired.'

His eyes on hers were dark and filled with intent. 'That's all? Just tired?'

For a moment she considered leaving it there. It had been a long day, but for the first time they seemed to be edging towards a calm she was reluctant to disturb. Although if she didn't tell him what she was really thinking, what would that achieve? Okay, it might just be one night in their lives, but if it was bothering her...bothering him...

She took a deep breath. 'I just want you to know that you don't have to take me to the party,' she said quickly.

His eyes narrowed. 'I know I don't. But I want to.' He studied her face. 'Is that really what this is about? What *I* want. Or is it about what *you* want?'

Nola looked at him uncertainly. 'What do you mean?'

He cleared his throat. 'Are you saying you don't want to go with me?'

She shook her head. 'No, but you only— I mean, your mother—'

He interrupted her, his voice suddenly blazing with an emotion she didn't recognise.

'Let me get one thing clear, Nola. *I want you to be there with me.* And my mother has got nothing to do with that decision.'

She nodded—for what else could she do? She could hardly demand proof. And she wanted to believe him. Of course she did. Besides, if they were going to work even at the simplest level, wasn't it time to move on? To put all the doubt and suspicion and drama behind them and start to trust one another?

Drawing in a deep breath, she lifted her chin and looked into his eyes.

'Thank you for telling me that,' she said simply. 'And thank you for taking me to lunch. It was lovely.' Remembering the strange tension around the table, those odd pointed remarks, she hesitated. 'What about you? Did you enjoy yourself?'

Ram stared at her in silence. Her question was simple enough but it stunned him, for he couldn't remember anyone ever asking him that before.

'I suppose,' he said finally. 'Although they were a little tense. But there's a lot going on—I mean, with the party coming up—'

She nodded slowly. 'Thirty years together is an amazing achievement.'

'Yes, it is.'

He watched her bite her lip, glance up, try to

speak, then look away. Finally she said quietly, 'I get that it's why you wanted me to meet them.'

His heart seemed to still in his chest. 'You do?'

She nodded. 'You wanted me to understand why you want us to marry. And I do understand. I know you want what they have.'

Her blue eyes were fixed on his face, and he stared back at her, his breath vibrating inside his chest.

You want what they have…

He tried to nod his head, tried to smile, to do what his mother had always required of him.

But he couldn't. Not anymore. Not with Nola.

Slowly he shook his head. 'Actually, what they have is why I've always been so *against* marriage.'

He watched her eyes widen with incomprehension, and it made him feel cruel—shattering her illusions, betraying his mother's confidences. But he was so tired of lying and feeling angry. His chest tightened. Nola deserved more than lies, more than his anger—she deserved the truth.

He cleared his throat. 'You see, Guy has a mistress.'

Confusion and shock spread out from her pupils like shock waves across a sea.

There was a thick, pulsing silence.

'But he can't have—' Nola bit her lip, stopped, tried again. 'Does your mother know?'

As she watched him nod slowly the room seemed to swim in front of her eyes.

There was another, shorter silence.

'I'm so sorry, Ram,' she whispered at last. 'That must have been such a shock.'

He stared past her, his eyes narrowing as though he was weighing something up.

'Yes, it was,' he said quietly. 'The first time it happened.'

The first time?

'I—I don't understand,' she said slowly. 'Isn't this the first time?'

His mouth twisted. 'Sadly not. That honour went to an actress called Francesca. Not that I knew or cared that she was an actress.' An ache of misery was spreading inside him. 'I was only six. To me, she was just some woman in my mother's bed.'

Nola flinched. *Six!* Still just a child.

Watching her reaction, Ram smiled stiffly. 'Guy told me it would upset my mother if I said anything. So I didn't.'

He was speaking precisely, owning each word in a way that made her feel sick.

'I thought if I kept quiet, then it would stop,' he continued. 'And it did with Francesca. Only then there was Tessa, and then Carrie. I stopped learning their names after that. It was the only way I could face my mother.'

'But you weren't responsible!' Nola stared up him, her eyes and her throat burning. 'You hadn't done anything.'

His skin was tight over his cheekbones.

'You're wrong. It *was* my fault. All of it.'

She shook her head. Her heart felt as if it was about to burst. 'You were a little boy. Your father should never have put you in that position.'

He was looking past her, his eyes dull with pain. 'You don't understand. *I'm* the reason they had to marry.'

She shivered. 'What do you mean?'

'My mother got pregnant with me when she was sixteen. In those days girls like her didn't do so well on their own.'

Nola blinked. She had imagined many reasons for what had made him the man he was, but nothing like this. No wonder he was so confused—and confusing—when it came to relationships.

'But that's not *your* fault,' she said quietly. 'I know it must have been hard for both of them. But just because Guy became a father too young, it doesn't mean you're responsible for his affairs.'

He shook his head, his mouth twisting into a smile that had nothing to do with laughter or happiness.

'Guy's not my father. My biological father, I mean.'

She stared at him in silence, too shocked to

speak, the words in her mouth bunching into silent knots.

He looked away. 'My mother was staying with a friend and they heard about a party. A real party, on the wrong side of town, with drink and boys and no supervision. That's where she met my father. They were drunk and careless and they had sex.'

'Who is he?' she whispered. 'Your real father?'

Ram shrugged. 'Does it matter? When he found out she was pregnant he didn't want anything to do with her—or me.'

His eyes were suddenly dark and hostile, as though challenging her to contradict him.

She swallowed. 'So how did she meet Guy?'

He breathed out unsteadily.

'My grandparents knew his family socially. His father had made some bad investments. Money was tight, and Guy's never been that interested in working for a living, so when Grandfather offered him money to marry my mother he accepted.'

Nola didn't even try to hide her shock.

'That's awful. Your poor mother. But why did she agree to it?'

Ram's face was bleak. 'Because my grandfather told her he'd cut her off, disown her, cast her out if she didn't.'

A muscle pulsed in his cheek.

'She couldn't face that, didn't think she could

survive without all this, so she gave in. Guy got a generous lifetime monthly allowance, my mother preserved her reputation and her lifestyle and my grandparents were able to keep their dirty linen private.'

The misery in his voice almost overwhelmed her.

She took a breath, counted to ten. 'How did you find out?'

'My mother told me.' This time his smile seemed to slice through her skin like a mezzaluna. 'We were arguing, and I compared her unfavourably to my grandparents. I hurt her, so I guess she thought it was time I knew the truth.'

Nola could feel her body shaking. How could his mother have done that? It had been needlessly cruel. She had to swallow hard against the tears building in her throat before she could speak.

'How old were you?'

He shrugged. 'Eleven…twelve, something like that.'

Her eyes held his as she struggled to think of something positive to say. 'But you get on with Guy?'

He shrugged. 'When I was a child he more or less ignored me. Now I'm older I just avoid him. After my grandfather died he made a big scene about needing more money, so I give him an allowance and in return he has to be devoted to my mother—in public, at least. And discreet about his affairs. Or he's supposed to be.'

Nola looked up into his face. There was nothing she could say to that.

'What about your real father?' she asked carefully. 'Do you have any contact with him?'

His eyes hardened. 'I know who he is, and since he knows who my mother is, he must know who *I* am, and how to find me. But he hasn't, so I guess he's even less interested in me than Guy.'

His face was expressionless but the desolation in his voice made her fists clench.

'It's his loss,' she said fiercely.

He gave a small, tight smile.

'Are you taking my side, Ms Mason?'

His words burned like a flame. Was she?

For months there had been an ocean between them. Then, for the last few days, she'd been fighting to keep him at a distance. Fighting to keep her independence. Fighting the simmering sexual tension between them. Her mouth twisted. In fact just fighting him.

Only now the fight had drained out of her, and instead she wanted nothing more than to wrap her arms around him, ease the desperate ache in his voice and that terrible tension in his body. Her breath seemed to swell in her throat as she reached out and tentatively touched his hand. For a moment he stared at her hand in silence, then finally he reached out and pulled her against him.

Burying her face against his body, she let out a shuddering breath. Being here in his arms felt so good, so right. If only she could stay this way for ever. But this wasn't about her, it was about Ram—*his* pain and his anger, his past. A past that still haunted him. A past she was determined to exorcise now.

Lifting her head, she looked up into his face. 'Your mother was so young. Too young. And she was scared and hurt and desperate. People don't always do the right thing when they're desperate. But they can do the wrong thing for the right reasons.'

Their eyes met, and they both knew she wasn't just talking about his mother.

Breathing out shakily, he shook his head. 'I've been struggling to figure that out for nearly twenty years. It's taken you less than half an hour.'

She smiled a little. 'It's all those in-flight magazines I read.'

Mouth twisting, he clasped her face, his thumbs gently stroking her cheeks.

'I'm sorry for what I did. Lying to you, dragging you off to the rainforest like that. It was completely out of order.'

Ram was apologising.

Her throat ached. She could hardly breathe.

'We both behaved badly,' she said shakily. 'And we both thought the worst of each other. But I'm glad you did what you did, otherwise we might never have got this far.'

Her gaze fastened on his face.

'But now we're here, and I think it's about time we started figuring things out. If we're going to make it work, I mean.'

The words were out of her mouth before she even understood what it was she wanted to say. What it was she really wanted. Her heart began to beat fiercely as his grey eyes searched her face.

'Make what work?'

It wasn't too late. There was still time to backtrack. Ram couldn't read minds, and she'd said nothing damning or definitive. But she didn't want to backtrack—for wasn't that their problem in a nutshell? Both of them looking back to the past, and in so doing threatening to ruin the future—their child's future? 'Our marriage,' she said after a moment.

'Are you asking me to marry you?'

He looked tense, shaken, nothing like the cool, sophisticated Ramsay Walker who could stop meetings with a raised eyebrow. It scared her a little, seeing him so uncertain. But it made her feel stronger, more determined to tell him how she felt—and maybe, just maybe, get him to do the same.

She hesitated. 'Yes, I am.'

He had confided in her, and she knew what each and every word had cost him. Knew too why he was so conflicted, so determined to do his duty as a father even as he pushed away any hint of love or commitment.

'Is this what's changed your mind?' he asked slowly.

She bit her lip. 'Yes, but also it was that night we spent in your office—I've tried not to think about it, but I can't stop myself. It was so different...so incredible. I've never felt like that with anyone, and I wanted to tell you that. I wanted to stay, but I was too scared—scared of how you'd made me feel.'

'I felt the same,' he said hoarsely.

She felt a sudden twinge of panic. 'But it was a long time ago. Maybe we don't feel that way anymore.'

His grey eyes locked onto hers.

'We do feel it, Nola. We've felt it and fought it.'

The heat in his voice made blood surge through her body.

'But I don't want to fight you anymore. In fact fighting is the opposite of what I want to do with you.'

She held her breath as he stared down into her eyes. Chaos was building inside her.

'What is it you want to do?' she whispered.

His gaze moved from her face down to the slight V of her cleavage.

'This...'

Holding her gaze, he reached out and slowly unwrapped the towel from around her body. As it dropped to the floor she heard his sharp intake of breath.

She swallowed, her imagination stirring.

His mouth was so close to hers—those beautiful curving lips that had the power to unleash a blissful torment of heat and oblivion. For a moment she couldn't speak. All she could think about was how badly she wanted to kiss him, and how badly she wanted him to kiss her back.

And then her breath lurched in her throat as, lowering his hand, he began stroking her breast in a way that made her quiver inside.

'I want you, Nola,' he said softly.

'For ever?' She couldn't help asking.

His gaze held hers, then his hands dipped lower to caress her stomach and her thighs and the curve of her bottom.

'For the rest of my life.'

She pressed her hands against his chest, feeling his heart beneath her fingertips, and then she was pushing him backwards onto the bed, and he was pulling her onto his lap so that she was straddling him.

Fingers trembling, she undid the button of his jeans, tugging at the zipper, freeing him. His ragged breathing abruptly broke the silence as she ran her hand gently up the length of him and guided him inside her.

He groaned, his body trembling. Leaning forward, she found his mouth and kissed him desperately. And then his hands were tightening on her thighs, and she was lifting her hips, heat swamping her as he shuddered inside her, pulling her damp, shaking body against his.

But it wasn't just desire that was rocking her body—it was shock. For mere sex, no matter how incredible, could not make you want to hold a person for ever.

Only love could make you feel that way.

It was like a dam breaking inside her, but even as she acknowledged the truth she knew it was not a truth she was ready to share with Ram. Or one he was ready to hear. But wrapped in his arms, with his heart beating in time with hers, it didn't seem to matter. For right now this was enough.

CHAPTER NINE

THE NEXT MORNING Ram woke early, to a sky of the palest blue and yellow.

Next to him Nola lay curled on her side, her arm draped across his chest. For a moment he lay listening to her soft, even breathing, his body and his brain struggling to adjust to this entirely new sensation of intimacy.

Waking beside a woman was something he'd never done before. In the past, even the thought of it would have made his blood run cold.

But being here with Nola felt good.

Better than good, he thought, breathing in sharply as she shifted against him in her sleep.

After last night there could be no doubt that they still wanted one another. They had made love slowly, taking their time, holding back and letting the pleasure build. And, unlike that first time in his office, there had been tenderness as well as passion.

Forehead creasing, he stared out of the window. But last night had not just been about sex. Exploring the lush new curves of her body had eased an ache that was more than physical.

He froze as Nola stirred beside him, curling closer, and suddenly the touch of her naked body was too great a test for his self-control. Gritting his teeth against the instant rush of need clamouring inside him, he gently lifted her arm and slid across the bed, making his way to the shower.

Turning the temperature to cool, he winced as the water hit his body.

For years he'd never so much as hinted at his parents' unhappiness to anyone. Even imagining the pity in someone's eyes had been enough to ensure his silence. But last night—and he still wasn't quite sure why or how—he'd ended up telling Nola every sordid little detail about his life. Not just his mother's miserable marriage of necessity, but Guy's serial affairs too.

The words had just tumbled out.

Only Nola hadn't pitied him. Instead she had helped him to face his past. More than that, she'd finally agreed to build a future with him.

Tipping back his head, he closed his eyes, remembering how she'd asked him to marry her. His mouth curved. Of course she had—and wasn't that as much of an attraction as her glorious body? The way she kept him guessing, and her stubborn determination to do things her way and at her pace.

Switching off the water, he smoothed his dark hair back against the clean lines of his skull. It ought to drive him crazy, yet it only seemed to intensify his desire for her. And now that Nola had finally come round to his point of view he was determined that nothing would get in their way.

Whatever it took, they were going to get married—and as soon as possible.

'I need to drop by the office later, so I was wondering if you'd like to go into town?'

They had just finished breakfast and Ram was flicking through some paperwork.

Looking over at him, Nola frowned. 'Is there a problem?'

He shook his head. 'I just need to show my face—otherwise there might be a mutiny.'

'I doubt that. Your staff love you.'

He laughed. '*Love* might be pushing it a little. They respect me—'

'Yes, and respect is a kind of love,' she said slowly. 'Like duty and faith. Love isn't just all about passion and romance—it's about commitment and consideration, and sacrifice too.'

He leaned back in his chair. 'Then I take it back. I must be very loved. So must you.'

She felt her skin grow hot. Of course he wasn't talking about their relationship but his staff, and probably her friendship with Anna. Aware, though, of his sudden focus, she grasped helplessly towards his earlier remark.

'When are you thinking of going into the office, then?'

'Whenever suits you.'

'In that case, maybe I'll stay here. It's not as if I really need anything.'

He was silent a moment, and then he said quietly, 'Apart from a dress?'

A dress?

She stared at him. 'Oh, yes, of course—for the party.'

His gaze rested on her face. 'Are you having second thoughts?'

His tone was relaxed, but there was an intensity in his grey eyes that made her heart beat faster.

'About the party?'

'About agreeing to marry me?'

Looking up, she shook her head. 'No. Are you?'

Gently he reached over and, smoothing her hair back from her face, he gave her one of those sweet, extraordinary smiles that could light up a room.

'If I could walk outside and find a registrar and a couple of witnesses, you'd be making an honest man out of me right this second!'

She burst out laughing. 'I thought the bride was supposed to be the pushy one?'

His face grew serious. 'I don't want to push you into anything, Nola. Not anymore. I just want you to give me a chance—to give us a chance.'

Heart bumping into her ribs, she nodded. 'I want that too.' Taking a quick breath, she smiled at him. 'So what happens next?'

There was a fraction of a pause.

'I suppose we make it official,' he said casually. 'How do you feel about announcing our engagement at the party?'

Her pulse darted forward. *Engagement?*

But of course logically their getting engaged was the next step.

Only up until yesterday marrying Ram had been more of a hypothetical option than a solid, nuts and bolts reality. And now he wanted to announce their engagement in three days.

Three days!

Ram watched with narrowed eyes as Nola bit her lip. Taking her to the party was a statement of sorts, but announcing their engagement there would escalate and consolidate their relationship in the most public way possible. Clearly Nola thought so too, for he could see the conflict in her eyes. Only instead of making him question his actions, her doubt and confusion only made him more determined than ever to make it happen.

But he'd learnt his lesson, and he wasn't about to make demands or start backing her into a corner.

'It does make sense,' she said finally.

And it did—but that didn't stop the feeling of dread rising up inside her. For how was everyone going to react to the news? Her heart gave a shiver. She might have finally come to terms with the idea of marrying Ram, but this was a reminder that their marriage was going to be conducted in public, with not only friends and family having an opinion but the media too.

'What is it?'

The unexpected gentleness of his voice caught her off guard, and quickly she looked away—for how could she explain her fears to him? Ram didn't know what it felt like to be hurt and humiliated in public, to have his failures held up and examined.

A lump filled her throat as she remembered the first time her father had let her down in front of other people. She'd been on a school trip, and he'd promised to collect her in his new car. She had been so convinced that he would pick her up, adamant that he wouldn't forget her. In the end one of the mothers had taken pity on her and driven her home, but of course the next day at school everyone had known.

She clenched her fists. And then there was what had happened with Connor. It had been bad enough splitting up with him. To do so under the microscope of her colleagues' curiosity and judgement had been excruciating.

Even thinking about it made her feel sick to her stomach.

She took a breath. 'It's just...once we tell everyone it won't be just the two of us anymore.'

'Yes—but, like I said, if we go to the party together then they'll know about us anyway.' He frowned. 'I'm confused—I thought you *wanted* to get married.'

'I do. But what if our marriage doesn't work?' The words were spilling out of her—hot, panicky, unstoppable. 'What happens then? Have you thought about that? Have you any idea what that will feel like—?'

She broke off as Ram reached out and covered her hands with his.

'Slow down, sweetheart. At this point I'm still trying to get you down the aisle. So right now I'm not thinking about the end of our marriage.'

Gently, he uncurled her fingers.

'Is this about your father?' he said quietly.

She shook her head, then nodded. 'Sort of. Him and Connor. He was my last boyfriend. We worked together. He told a couple of people in the office some stuff about us, and then it all got out of hand.'

'What stuff? And what do you mean by "out of hand"?'

She couldn't meet his eyes. 'Some of my colleagues went to the pub after work. Connor had been drinking, and he told them—well, he told them things about us. You know…what we'd done together, private things. The next day everyone was talking about me. It was so embarrassing.

Even my boss knew. People I thought were my friends stopped talking to me, I was overlooked for a promotion, and then Connor dumped me.'

'Then, quite frankly, he was an idiot,' Ram said bluntly. Cupping her chin in his hand, he forced her face up to his. 'Correction. He's an idiot and a coward, and if ever I meet him I'll tell him so— shortly after I've punched him.'

She couldn't stop herself from smiling. 'You don't need to worry about me. I can fight my own battles.'

His gaze rested on her face, and he gripped her hand so tightly she could almost feel the energy and strength passing from his body into hers.

'Not anymore. You're with me now, Nola. Your battles are my battles. And, engaged or not, nothing anyone says or does is going to change that fact, so if you don't want to say anything, then we won't.'

Nola stared at him in silence. She knew how badly he wanted to get married, but he was offering to put his needs and feelings behind hers. Neither her father nor Connor had been willing to do that.

She couldn't speak—not just because his words had taken her by surprise, but because she was terrified she would tell him that she loved him.

Finally, she shook her head. 'I do want to announce it. But I think I should ring my mum and

Anna first. I want them to know before anyone else.'

He dropped a kiss on her mouth. 'Good idea. Why don't you call them now? And then you'd better come into town with me after all, so you can choose a dress.'

It was the afternoon of the party.

Slipping her feet into a pair of beautiful dark red court shoes, Nola breathed out softly. She could hardly believe that in the next few hours she would be standing beside Ram as his fiancée. Just days ago they had been like two boxers, circling one another in the ring. But all that had changed since they'd made peace with their pasts, and she had never felt happier.

Or more satisfied.

Her face grew hot. It was crazy, but they just couldn't seem to keep their hands off one another. Even when they weren't making love they couldn't stop touching—his hand on her hip, her fingers brushing against his face. And on the odd occasion when she forced Ram to do some work he'd stay close to her, using his laptop and making phone calls from the bed while she slept.

In fact this was probably the first time they'd been apart for days, and she was missing him so badly that it felt like an actual physical ache.

Her breath felt blunt and heavy in her throat. It

was an ache that was compounded by the knowledge that, even though she loved him, Ram would never love her. She lifted her chin. But he did *need* her, and he felt responsible for her and the baby—and hadn't she told him that duty was a kind of love?

But she couldn't think about that now. There were other more pressing matters to consider and, heart pounding, she turned to face the full-length mirror. She stared almost dazedly at her reflection. It was the first time she had seen herself since having her hair and make-up done, and the transformation was astonishing. With her dark hair swept to one side, her shimmering smoky eye make-up and bright red lips, she looked poised and glamorous—not at all like the anxious young woman she was feeling inside.

Which was lucky, she thought, picking up her clutch bag with a rush of nervous excitement, because soon she would be facing Sydney's A-listers as Ram's bride-to-be.

Downstairs, Ram was flicking resignedly through the pages of a magazine. If Nola was anything like Pandora he was going to be in for a long wait. Or maybe he wasn't! Already Nola had surprised him, by being sweetly excited by the party, whereas Pandora was just too much of a perfectionist to truly enjoy *any* public appearance. She saw only the flaws, however tiny or trifling. And of course that led inevitably to the reasons for those flaws.

His mouth tightened. Or rather *the* reason.

There was a movement behind him and, turning round, he felt his heartbeat stumble.

Nola was standing at the top of the stairs, wearing a beautiful pleated yellow silk dress that seemed to both cling and flow. It perfectly complemented her gleaming dark hair and crimson lips and, watching her walk towards him, he felt his breath catch fire as she stopped in front of him. She met his gaze, her blue eyes nervous, yet resolute.

'You look like sunlight in that dress,' he said softly and, reaching out he pulled her towards him. 'You're beautiful, Nola. Truly.'

'You look pretty damn spectacular too,' she said huskily.

The classic black dinner jacket fitted his muscular frame perfectly, and although all the male guests at the party would be similarly dressed, she knew that beside Ram they would look ordinary. His beauty and charisma would ensure that.

He glanced down at himself, then up to her face, his grey gaze dark and mocking. 'I doubt anyone's going to be looking at me.'

She shivered. 'Hopefully they won't be looking at me either.'

'They can look. But they can't touch.'

His arm tightened around her waist and she saw that his eyes were no longer mocking but intent and alert. Tipping her chin up, he cupped her face in his hand.

'You're mine. And I want everyone to know that. After tonight, they will.'

She felt her heart slip sideways, like a boat breaking free from its moorings. But of course he was just getting into the mood for the evening ahead, and it was her cue to do the same.

'I'll remind you of that later, when we're dancing and I'm trampling on your toes,' she said lightly. 'You'll be begging other men to take me off your hands.'

His face shifted, the corners of his mouth curving upwards, and his arms held her close against him.

'And what will you be begging *me* to do?'

Their eyes met, and she felt her face grow warm. She hadn't begged yet, but she hadn't been far off it. Remembering how frantic she had felt last night, how desperate she had been for his touch, the frenzy of release, she swallowed.

'We shouldn't—'

He nodded. 'I know. I just wish we could fast-forward tonight.'

She could hear the longing in his voice. 'So do I. I wish it was just the two of us.'

'It will be.' He frowned. 'I know you're nervous. But I'll be there with you, and if for some reason I'm not—well, I thought this might help. I hope you like it.'

He lifted her hand and Nola stared mutely as he slid a beautiful sapphire ring onto her finger.

A sweet, shimmering lightness began to spread through her body. 'It—It's a ring,' she stammered.

His eyes glittered. 'You sound surprised. What were you expecting?'

'Nothing. I wasn't expecting anything.'

'We're getting engaged tonight, sweetheart. There has to be a ring.'

She nodded, some of her happiness fading. He was right: there did have to be a ring.

'Of course,' she said quickly. 'And it's lovely. Really…'

'Good.' Pulling out his phone, he glanced down at the screen and grimaced. 'In that case, I guess we should be going.'

Bypassing the queue of limousines and sports cars in the drive, Ram used the service entrance to reach the house. As they walked hand in hand towards the two huge marquees on the lawn Nola shivered. There were so many guests—several hundred at least.

'Do your parents really know this many people?' she asked, gazing nervously across the lawn.

He shrugged. 'Socially, yes. Personally, I doubt

they could tell you much more than their names and which clubs they belong to.'

He turned as a waiter passed by with a tray of champagne and grabbed two glasses.

'I'm not drinking.'

'I know. But just hold it—otherwise somebody will wonder why.'

He smiled down at her and she nodded dumbly. He was so aware, so in control of everything. In that respect this evening was no different for him than any other.

If only she could let him know how different it was for *her*.

But, much as she longed to tell him that she loved him, she knew it wasn't the right time. For there was a tension about him, a remoteness, as though he was holding himself apart. It was the same tension she'd felt at lunch that day with his parents. And of course it was understandable. This was a big moment for him too.

The party passed in a blur of lights and faces. She knew nobody, but it seemed that everybody knew Ram, and so wanted to know her too. Clutching her glass of champagne, she smiled and chatted with one glamorous couple after another as Ram stood by her side, looking cool and absurdly handsome in his tuxedo as he talked in French to a tall, elderly grey-haired man who turned out to be the Canadian Ambassador.

Later, ignoring her protests, he led her onto the dance floor and, holding her against his body, he circled her between the other couples.

'Are you having fun?' he said softly into her ear.

She nodded. 'Yes. I thought people might be a bit stiff and starchy. But everyone's been really friendly.'

His eyes glittered like molten silver beneath the soft lights. 'They like you.'

She shook her head. 'They're curious about me. It's *you* they like.'

'And what about you? Do *you* like me?'

Around them the music and the laughter seemed to fade, as though someone had turned down the volume, and the urge to tell him her true feelings welled up inside her again. But she bit it down.

She smiled. 'Yes, I like you.'

'And you still want to marry me?' He met her gaze, his grey eyes oddly serious. 'It's not too late to change your mind…'

She shook her head. 'I want to marry you.'

'Then maybe now is a good time to tell everyone that.' Glancing round, he frowned. 'We need my parents here, though. Let's go and look for them.'

His hand was warm and firm around hers as he pulled her through the dancing couples and onto the lawn, but after ten minutes of looking they still hadn't found Guy and Pandora.

Nodding curtly at the security guards, he led her into the main house.

'My mother probably wanted to change her shoes or something. I'll go and find them.'

His eyes were fixed on her face and, seeing the hesitancy there, she felt her heart tumble inside her chest.

Taking his hands in hers, she gave them a squeeze. 'Why don't I come with you? We can tell them together.'

There was a brief silence as he stared away across the empty hallway. Then his mouth twisted, and he shook his head. 'It's probably better if I go on my own.'

She nodded. 'Okay. I'll wait here.'

He kissed her gently on the lips. 'I won't be long.'

Walking swiftly through the house, Ram felt his heart start to pound.

He could hardly believe he'd managed to get this far. Bringing Nola to the party had felt like a huge step but this—this was something almost beyond his comprehension, beyond any expectations he'd had up until now.

It hardly seemed possible, but by the end of the night he would be officially engaged to Nola. Finally, with her help, he had managed to bury his past, and now he had a future he'd never imagined, with a wife and a baby—

Abruptly, his feet stilled on the thick carpet and his thoughts skidded forward, slamming into the side of his head with a sickening thud.

His heartbeat froze. Beneath the throb of music and laughter, he could hear raised voices. Somewhere in the house a man and woman were arguing loudly.

It was Guy and his mother.

His heart began beating again and, with the blood chilling in his veins, he walked towards the doorway to his mother's room. The voices grew louder and more unrestrained as he got closer.

And then he heard his mother laugh.

Only it wasn't a happy sound.

'You just can't help yourself, can you? Couldn't you have a little self-control? Just for one night?'

'Maybe you should have a little *less*, darling. It's a party—not a military tattoo.'

Ram winced. Guy sounded belligerent. And drunk.

For a moment he hesitated. There had been so many of these arguments during his life. Surely it wouldn't matter if he walked away from this one? But as his mother started to cry he braced his shoulders and walked into the bedroom.

'Oh, here's the cavalry.' Turning, Guy squinted across the room at him. 'Don't start, Ram. You don't pay me enough to take part in that gala performance downstairs.'

'But I pay you enough to treat my mother with respect,' he said coolly. 'However, if you don't think you can manage to do that, maybe I'll just have to cut back your allowance. No point in paying for something I'm not actually getting.'

For a moment Guy held his gaze defiantly, but then finally he shrugged and looked away. 'Fine. But if you think I'm going to deal with her in this state—'

'I'll deal with my mother.' Ram forced himself to stay calm. 'Why don't you go and enjoy the party? Eat some food…have a soft drink. Oh, and Guy? I meant what I said about treating my mother with respect.'

Grumbling, still avoiding Ram's eyes, Guy stumbled from the room.

Heart aching, Ram stared across the room to where his mother sat crying on the bed. Crossing the room, he crouched down in front of her and stroked her hair away from her face.

'Don't worry about him. He's been drinking, that's all. And he's had to get up before noon to make a couple of phone calls so he's probably exhausted.'

She tried to smile through her tears. 'That must be it.'

'It is. Now, here. Take this.' Reaching into his pocket, Ram pulled out a handkerchief and held it out to her. 'It's clean. I promise.'

Taking the handkerchief, Pandora wiped her eyes carefully. 'I just wanted it to be perfect, Ramsay. For one night.'

'And it is. Everyone's having a wonderful time.'

She shook her head, pressing her hand against his. '*You're* not. You'll say you are, but I know you're not.'

Ram swallowed. Whenever his mother and Guy argued there was a pattern. She would get angry, then cry, and then she would redo her make-up and carry on as if nothing had happened. But tonight was different, for he could never remember her talking about him or his feelings.

He looked at her uncertainly. 'You're right—normally. But it's different tonight. I really am enjoying myself.'

His mother smiled.

'That's because of Nola. *She's* the difference and you're different with her. Happier.' She squeezed his hand. 'I was happy like that when I found out I was pregnant with you. I know it sounds crazy, but when that line turned blue I just sat and looked at it, and those few hours when it was just you and me were the happiest of my life. I knew then that you'd be handsome and smart and strong.'

A tear rolled down her cheek.

'I just wish I'd been stronger.'

Ram dragged a hand through his hair. He felt her pain like a weight. 'You *were* strong, Mother.'

Shaking her head, she let the tears fall. 'I should never have married Guy. I should have had the courage to stand up to your grandfather. I should have waited for someone who wanted me and loved me for who I was.'

Looking up into Ram's eyes, she twisted her lips.

'But I was scared to give all this up. So I settled for a man who was paid to marry me and a marriage that's made me feel trapped and humiliated for thirty years.'

She bit her lip.

'I'm sorry, darling, for acting so selfishly, and for blaming you.'

Ram couldn't breathe.

His mother was apologising.

For so long he'd been so angry with her. Never to her face, because despite everything—the hysterics, the way she lashed out at him when she was upset—he loved her desperately. Instead he'd deliberately, repeatedly, and publicly scorned the very idea of becoming a husband and a father.

And he'd done that to punish her. For giving him a 'father' like Guy, for making choices that had taken away *his* choices, even though she'd been little more than a child herself.

'Don't,' he whispered. 'It wasn't your father.'

'It was. It *is*.' Reaching out, Pandora gently stroked his face. 'And I can't change the past. But I don't want you to repeat my mistakes. Promise me, Ramsay, that you won't do what Guy and I did. Relationships can't be forced. There has to be love.'

'I know.'

He spoke mechanically, but inside he felt hollow, for he knew his mother was right. Relationships couldn't be forced—and yet wasn't that exactly what he'd done to Nola? Right from the start he'd been intent on having his own way—overriding her at every turn, kidnapping her at the airport, pressuring her to get married.

He'd even 'persuaded' her into announcing their engagement tonight, despite knowing that she was nervous about taking that step.

His breath felt like lead in his throat. Whatever he might like to believe, the facts were undeniable. Nola wasn't marrying him through choice or love. Just like his mother, for her it would be a marriage of convenience. A marriage of duty.

Gazing into his mother's tear-stained face, he made up his mind.

He'd never wanted anything more than to give his child a secure home, a future, a name. But he couldn't marry Nola.

Now all he needed to do was find her and tell her that as soon as possible.

Glancing up, Nola saw Ram striding down the stairs towards her. Her heart gave a lurch. He didn't look as if news of his engagement had been joyfully received.

Standing up, she walked towards him—but before she had a chance to speak Ram was by her side, grabbing her hand, towing her after him, his grip on her hand mirroring the vice of confusion and fear squeezing her heart.

'What did they say?' she managed as he wrenched open the door, standing to one side to let her pass through it.

'Nothing,' he said curtly. 'I didn't tell them.'

She gazed at him in confusion.

'So what are we doing?'

'There's been a change of plan. We're leaving now!'

Five minutes later they were heading down the drive towards the main road. Cars were still arriving at the house, but even though Ram must have noticed them, he said nothing.

Several times she was on the verge of asking him to stop the car and tell her what had happened. But, glancing at his set, still profile, she knew that he was either incapable of telling her or unwilling. All she could do was watch and wait.

She was so busy watching him that she didn't even notice when they drove past Stanmore. In fact it wasn't until he stopped the car in front of a large Art Deco–style house that she finally became aware of anything other than the terrible rigidity of his body.

He had switched off the engine and was out of the car and striding round to her door, yanking it open before she even had a chance to take off her seatbelt.

'This way!'

Taking her hand, he led her to the front door, unlocking and opening it in one swift movement. Inside the house, Nola watched confusedly as he marched from room to room, flicking on lights.

'What is this place?' she said finally.

'It's a property I bought a couple of years ago as an investment. I lived here when Stanmore was being renovated.'

'Oh, right...' It was all she could manage.

Maybe this was some kind of bolthole? She flinched as he yanked the curtains across the windows. If so, he must have a good reason for coming here now. But as she stared over at him anxiously she had no idea what that reason might be. All she knew was that she wanted to put her arms around him and hold him tight. Only, he looked so brittle, so taut, she feared he might shatter into a thousand pieces if she so much as touched him.

But she couldn't just stand here and pretend that everything was all right when it so clearly wasn't.

'Are you okay?' she asked hesitantly.

'Yes. I'm fine.'

He smiled—the kind of smile she would use when sharing a lift with a stranger.

'I'm sure you're tired. Why don't I show you to your bedroom?'

'But don't you want to talk?'

Watching his expression shift, she shivered. It was like watching water turn to ice.

'No, not really.'

'But what happened? Why did we leave the party?' She bit her lip. 'Why didn't you tell them about the engagement?'

He stared at her impatiently, then fixed his eyes on a point somewhere past her head.

'I'm not having this conversation now. It's late. You're pregnant—'

'And you're upset!' She stared at him in exasperation. 'Not only that, you're shutting me out.'

His eyes narrowed. 'Shutting you out? You sound like you're in a soap opera.'

She blinked, shocked not so much by his words but by the sneer in his voice.

'Maybe that's because you've behaving like a character in a soap opera. Dragging me from the party. Refusing to talk to me.'

'And what exactly do you think talking about it will achieve?'

'I don't know.' Her breath felt tight inside her chest. 'But I don't think ignoring whatever it is can be the solution.'

He gave a short, bitter laugh. 'You've changed your tune. Not so long ago you managed to ignore me for three months without much problem.'

Nola felt her whole body tighten with shock and pain. Then, almost in the same moment, she knew he was lashing out at her because he was upset, and even though his words hurt her she cared more about *his* pain than her own.

'And I was wrong.'

'So maybe in three months I'll think I was wrong about this. But somehow I don't think so.'

She gritted her teeth. 'So that's it? You just want me to shut up and go to bed?'

His face hardened. 'No, what I want is for you to stop nagging me, like the wife you've clearly never wanted to be.'

'I *do* want to be your wife.' The injustice of his words felt like a slap. 'And I'm not nagging. I'm trying to have a conversation.'

He shook his head. 'This isn't a conversation. It's an interrogation.'

'Then *talk* to me.'

His jaw tightened. 'Fine. I was going to wait until the morning, but if you can't or won't wait, we'll do it now.'

'Do what?'

'Break up. Call it off.' His voice was colder and harder than his gaze. 'Whatever one does to end an engagement.'

Watching the colour drain from her face, he felt

sick. But knowing that he could hurt her so easily only made him more determined to finish it there and then—for what was the alternative? That she spent the next thirty years trapped with him in a loveless marriage?

A marriage that would force their child to endure the same dark legacy as him.

No, that wasn't going to happen. His child deserved more than to be a witness to his parents' unhappy marriage. And Nola deserved more than him.

Across the room Nola took a breath, tried to focus, to make sense of what Ram had just said.

'I don't understand,' she said finally.

But then, staring at him, she did—for the man who had held her in his arms and made love to her so tenderly had been replaced by a stranger with blank, hostile eyes.

'You want to end our engagement? But you were going to announce it tonight...'

He shrugged. 'And now I'm not.'

But I love you, she thought, her heart banging against her ribcage as though it was trying to speak for itself. Only it was clear that Ram had no use for her love, for any kind of love.

'Why?' she whispered. 'Why are you doing this?'

'I've changed my mind. All this—us, marriage, becoming a father—it's not what I want.'

'But you said that children need to know where

they come from. That they need to belong.' His words tasted like ash in her mouth.

His gaze locked onto hers. 'Don't look so surprised, Nola. You said yourself I'm not cut out to be a hands-on daddy. And you're right. I'm not. What was it you said? No father is better than a bad father. Well, you were right. You'll do a far better job on your own than with me messing up your life and our child's life. But you don't need to worry. I fully intend to take care of you and the baby financially.'

Nola stared at him in silence.

He was talking in the same voice he used for board meetings. In fact he might just as easily have been discussing an upcoming software project instead of his child.

Her heart was beating too fast. Misery and anger were tangling inside her chest.

'Is that what you think matters?' she asked, reining in her temper.

He sighed. 'Try not to let sentiment get in the way of reason. Everything that baby needs is going to cost money so, yes, I think it *does* matter.'

'Not everything,' she said stubbornly. 'Children need love, consistency, patience and guidance, and all those are free.'

His mouth curled. 'Tell that to a divorce lawyer.'

Reaching into his pocket, he pulled out his car keys.

'There's no point in discussing this now. You can stay here, and I'll call my lawyers in the morning. I'll get them to draw up the paperwork and they can transfer this house into your name tomorrow.'

'What?' She stared at him, struggling to breathe.

'I'll work out a draft financial settlement at the same time. As soon as that's finalised we can put all this behind us and get back to our lives.'

Her skin felt cold, but she was burning up inside.

So was that it? Everything she had been through, that *they* had been through, had been for this? For him to pay her off. Just like her father had done with his ostentatious but impersonal presents.

Anger pounded through her. And, just like those presents, giving her this house and an allowance were for *his* benefit, not hers. He was offering them as a means to assuage his conscience and rectify the mistake he clearly believed he'd made by getting her pregnant.

'I don't want your house or your money,' she said stiffly.

He frowned. 'Please don't waste my time, or yours, making meaningless remarks like that. You're going to need—'

She shook her head. 'No, you don't get to offer me money. Aside from my salary, I've never asked for or expected any money from you, and nothing's changed.'

His eyes narrowed. 'Give it time.'

She felt sick—a sickness that was worse than anything she'd felt in those early months of pregnancy. For that nausea had been caused by the child growing inside her, a child she loved without question, even when she felt scared and alone.

Now, though, she felt sick at her own stupidity.

Ignoring all her instincts, she had let herself have hope, let herself trust him. Not just trust him—but love him too.

And here was the proof that she'd been wrong all along.

Ram was just like her father, for when it came to sacrificing himself for his family he couldn't do it.

He was weak and selfish and he was not fit to be a father to her child.

Wide-eyed, suddenly breathless with anger, Nola stepped forward, her fingers curling into fists.

'Get out! You can keep your stupid financial settlements and your paperwork. As of this moment I never want to see or speak to you again, Ramsay Walker. Now, get out!'

He stared at her in silence, then, tossing the house keys onto one of the tables, he turned and walked swiftly across the room.

The door slammed and moments later she heard his car start, the engine roaring in the silence of the night and then swiftly fading away until the only sound was her ragged breathing.

It was then that she realised she was still wearing his ring. Unclenching her fingers, she gazed down at the sapphire, thinking how beautiful it was, and yet how sad.

And then her legs seemed to give way beneath her and, sliding down against the wall, she began to sob.

CHAPTER TEN

FINALLY IT WAS time to stop crying.

Forcing herself to stand up, Nola walked into the kitchen and splashed her face with cold water. Her mascara had run, and she wiped it carefully away with her fingertips. But as she tried to steady her breathing she knew it would be a long time—and take a lot more than water—to wash away Ram's words or that look on his face.

Her chest tightened, and suddenly the floor seemed to be moving. She gripped the edge of the sink.

Ram giving up like that had been so shocking—brutal, and cruel.

Like a bomb exploding.

And she still didn't really understand what had happened to make him change his mind—not just about the engagement but about everything. For her, cocooned in her newly realised love, it had begun to feel as though finally there was a future for them.

She felt anger scrape over her skin.

But what use was love to a man like Ram?

A man who measured his feelings in monthly maintenance payments?

Steadying herself, she lifted her shoulders. She

wasn't going to fall apart. For what had she really lost?

Even before she'd thrown him out she had felt as though the Ram she loved had already left. He'd been so remote, so cold, so ruthless. Changing his mind, her life, her future and their child's future without batting an eyelid, then offering her money as some kind of consolation prize.

Her throat tightened, and suddenly she was on the verge of tears again.

And now he was gone.

And she knew that she would never see him again.

Somewhere in the house a clock struck two, and she felt suddenly so tired and drained that standing was no longer an option. There were several sofas in the living room, but she knew that if she sat down she would never get up again, and lying on a sofa in a party dress seemed like the worst kind of defeat. If she was going to sleep, she was going to do it in a bed.

Slipping off her shoes, she walked wearily upstairs. There was no shortage of bedrooms—she counted at least seven—but as she opened one door after another she began to feel like Goldilocks. Each room was beautiful, but the beds were all too huge, too empty for just her on her own.

Except that she wasn't on her own, she thought defiantly, stroking the curve of her stomach with her hand. Nor was she going to lie there worrying about the future. Her mother had more or less brought her up on her own and, unlike her mother, *she* was financially independent. So, with or without Ram, she was going to survive this *and* flourish.

Getting undressed seemed like too much of an effort, though, and, stifling a yawn, she crawled onto the next bed and slid beneath the duvet.

She didn't remember falling asleep, but when she opened her eyes she felt sure that she must have dozed off only for a couple of minutes. But one glance at the clock on the bedside table told her that she had been asleep for two hours.

Her skin felt tight from all the crying, and her head was pounding—probably from all the crying too. Feeling a sudden terrible thirst, she sat up and wriggled out from under the duvet.

The house was silent and still, but she had left some of the lights on during her search for a bedroom. Squinting against the brightness, she made her way towards the stairs. It was dark in the living room, but her head was still so muddied with sleep that it was only as she began to grope for a light switch that she remembered she had also left the lights on downstairs.

So why were they off now?

In the time it took for her heart to start beating

again she had already imagined several nightmare crazed intruder scenarios—and then something, or someone, moved in the darkness and her whole body seemed to turn to lead.

'It's okay…it's just me.'

A lamp flared in the corner of the room, but she didn't need it to know that it was Ram sitting in one of the armchairs. She would recognise that voice anywhere—even in darkness. And even had he lost his voice she would still have known him, for she had traced the pure, straight line of his jaw with her fingers. Touched those firm, curving lips with her mouth.

She felt a sudden sharp stab of desire, remembering the way his body had moved against hers. Remembering too how much she'd loved him. How much she still loved him. But with loving came feelings, and she wasn't going to let herself feel anything for this man anymore, or give him yet another chance to hurt her.

'How did you get in?' she asked stiffly.

'I have a spare key.'

Her heart began to race with anger, for his words had reminded her of the promise he'd made only a few hours ago. Not to love her and his child, but to take care of them financially, provide a fitting house and lifestyle.

Glancing round, she spotted the keys he'd left

behind earlier, and with hands that shook slightly she picked them up.

'Here, you can have these too.' She tossed them to him. 'Since I'm not planning on staying here I won't be needing them. In fact...' She paused, tugging at the ring on her finger. 'I won't be needing this either.'

'Nola, please—don't do that.' He struggled to his feet, his mouth twisting.

'Don't do *what*, Ramsay?' She stared at him, a cloud of disbelief and anger swirling inside her. 'Why are you even here? I told you I never wanted to see you again.'

'I know. But you also said that ignoring this wasn't the solution.'

His voice was hoarse, not at all like his usual smooth drawl, but she was too strung out to notice the difference.

'Well, I was wrong. Like I was wrong to give you a chance. And wrong to think that you'd changed, that you could change.' Meeting his gaze, she said quickly, 'I know I've made a lot of mistakes, but I'm not about to repeat them by wasting any more of my time on you, so I'd like you to leave now.'

He sucked in a breath, but didn't move. 'I can't do that. I know you're angry, but I'm not leaving until you've listened to me.'

Her eyes widened, the pulse jerking in her

throat. She didn't want to listen to anything he had to say, but she could tell by the set of his shoulders that he had meant what he said. He was just going to stand there and wait—stand there and wait for her to grow tired of fighting him and give in. Just as she always did, she thought angrily.

Blood was beating in her ears.

Taking a step backwards, she folded her arms protectively around her waist and looked at him coldly. 'Then say whatever it is and then I want you to leave.'

Ram stared at her in silence.

Her face was pale and shadowed. She was still wearing her dress from last night, and he knew that she must have slept in it, for it was impossibly crumpled now. But he didn't think she had ever looked more beautiful, or desirable, or determined.

Or that he had ever loved her more.

He stood frozen, his body still with shock. But inside the truth tugged him down and held him fast, like an anchor digging into the seabed.

He loved her.

He hadn't planned to. Or wanted to. But he knew unquestioningly that it was true.

And, crazy though it sounded, he knew it was the reason he'd broken up with her.

He'd told himself—told her—that he had never wanted to marry or have children. That he wasn't a good bet. That he would only ruin everything. And all of that had been true.

But it wasn't the whole truth.

He loved her, and in loving her he couldn't force her into a marriage of convenience. For, even though she had agreed to be his wife, he knew that she didn't love him. And he'd seen with his own eyes the damage and misery that kind of relationship could cause. He only had to look at his mother or look in the mirror for proof.

No, he didn't wanted to trap her—only he couldn't bear a life without Nola, a life without his child.

But how he could salvage this?

He took a deep breath. 'I know I've messed up. And I know you don't have any reason to listen to me, let alone forgive me, but I want a second chance. I want us to try again.'

For a moment she couldn't understand what he was saying, for it made no sense. Only a couple of hours ago he had said that he wanted to break up with her, to go back to his old life, and yet now he was here, asking her for a second chance.

But even as her brain raged against the inconsistency of his words her heart was responding to the desperation in his voice.

Only she couldn't do this again. Couldn't start to believe, to hope.

Ignoring the ache in her chest, she shook her

head. '*You* gave up on *me*. And on our baby. Or have you forgotten that you were supposed to announce our engagement last night—?' She broke off, her voice catching in her throat as pain split her in two.

He took a step towards her, and for the first time it occurred to her that he looked as desperate as he sounded. There were shadows under his eyes and he was trembling all over.

'I haven't forgotten, and I'm sorry—'

'You're *sorry*!'

She shook her head. Did he really think that saying sorry was somehow going to make everything right again? If so, she had been right to throw him out.

'Well, don't be—I'm not. You know what? I'm *glad* you broke it off, because there's something wrong with you. Something that means that every time we get to a place of calm and understanding you have to smash it all to pieces. And I can't—I don't want to live like that.'

'I know, and I don't want to live like that either.'

He sounded so wretched. But why should she care? In fact she wasn't going to care, she told herself.

Only it was so hard, for despite her righteous anger she still loved him. But thankfully he would never know that.

'Then it's lucky for both of us that we don't

have to,' she said quickly. 'As soon as I can get a flight back to Scotland I'm going home.'

She watched as he took a deep breath, and the pain in his eyes tugged at an ache inside her, so that suddenly she could hardly bear looking at his stricken face.

'But this is your home...'

She shook her head. 'It's *not* my home. It's a pay-off. A way for you to make yourself feel better. I don't want it.'

Ram stared at her in silence. The blood was roaring in his ears.

He was losing her. He was losing her.

The words echoed inside his head and he could hardly speak through the grief rising up in his throat. 'But I want you. And I want to marry you.'

Her heart began to beat faster. It was so tempting to give in, for she knew that right now he believed what he was saying. But now was just a moment in time: it wouldn't last for ever. And she was done with living in the moment.

Slowly she shook her head. 'Only because you can't have me. I don't know *what* you want, Ram. But I do know that you can't just break up with me and then two hours later come and tell me that you want me back and expect everything to be okay again. Maybe if this was a film we could kiss, and then the credits would roll, and everyone in the cinema would go home happy. But we're *not* in a film. This is real life, and it doesn't work like that.'

Tears filled her eyes.

'You hurt me, Ram…' she whispered.

'I know.'

The pain in his voice shocked her.

'I wish I could go back and change what I did and what I said. I panicked. When I went to find my mother she told me not to make the same mistake that she had. That relationships can't be forced. That they need love. That's why I couldn't go through with it.'

She nodded. 'Because you don't love me—I know,' she said dully.

'No!' He let out a ragged breath. 'I broke up with you because I *do* love you, Nola, and I didn't want to trap you in a marriage that you didn't want. That you never wanted.'

He took a step towards her, his hands gripping her arms, his eyes glittering not with tears but with passion.

'I *love* you, and that's why I want to marry you. Not out of duty, or because I want the baby to have my name. But I know you don't love me, and I've hurt you so much already. Only I couldn't just walk away. I tried, but I couldn't do it. That's why I came back—'

He stopped. There were tears in her eyes.

Only she was smiling.

'You love me? *You love me?*'

He stared at her uncertainly, his eyes burning, wishing there was another way to tell her that—to make her believe. But even before he'd started to nod she was pressing her hand against her mouth, as though that would somehow stop the tears spilling from her eyes.

'You're so smart, Ram. Easily the smartest person I've ever met. But you're also the stupidest. *Why* do think I agreed to marry you?'

'I don't know...' he whispered.

'Because I love you, of course.'

Gazing up into his face, Nola felt her heart almost stop beating as she saw that he too was crying.

'Why would you ever love me?'

His voice broke apart and she felt the crack inside her deepen as his mouth twisted in pain.

'How could you love me? After everything I've said and done? After how I've behaved?'

'I don't know.' She bit her lip. 'I didn't want to. And it scares me that I do. But I can't help it. I love you.' Her mouth trembled. 'I love you and I still want to marry you.'

His hands tightened around her arms, his eyes searching her face. 'Are you sure? I don't want to trap you. I don't want to be that kind of man—that kind of husband, that kind of father.'

Her heart began to beat faster. 'You're not. Not anymore. I don't think you ever were.'

Breathing out unsteadily, he pulled her close, smoothing the tears away from her face. 'Your parents married because it was the next step,' he said slowly. 'My mother married Guy out of desperation. They didn't think about what they were doing…it just happened. But we're different. We've fought to be together, and our marriage is going to work just fine.'

She breathed out shakily. 'How do you know?'

His eyes softened. 'Because you know me,' he said simply. 'You know everything about me—the good and the bad. And you still love me.'

Her lip trembled. 'Yes, I do.'

'It scares me, you knowing me like that.' He grimaced. 'But I trust you, and I love you, and I always will.'

Gently, he uncurled her arms from around her body, and as one they stepped towards each other.

Burying her face against his chest, Nola sighed with relief as Ram pulled her close.

'I love you, Nola.'

She lifted her head. 'I love you too.'

For several minutes they held each other in silence, neither wanting to let go of the other, to let go of what they had come so close to losing.

Finally Ram shifted backwards. 'Do you think it's too late to tell my mother?'

Tracing the curve of his mouth with her fingers, she laughed. 'I think it might be better for us to get some sleep first. Besides, what's a couple of hours when we have the rest of our lives together?'

'The rest of our lives together…' He repeated it softly, and then laying one hand across the swell of her stomach, he pulled her closer still, so that he and Nola and the baby were all connected. 'That's a hell of a future,' he whispered, kissing her gently on the forehead.

Looking up into his handsome face, Nola felt her heart swell with happiness. All the hardness and anger had gone and there was only hope and love in his grey eyes.

'Although, from where I'm standing, the present looks pretty damn good too.'

She bit her lip, her mouth curling up at the corners. 'I think it would look even better lying down.'

'My thoughts exactly,' he murmured, and with his heart beating with love and joy he scooped her up into his arms and carried her towards the stairs.

EPILOGUE

STEPPING UNDER THE shower head, Nola switched on the water and closed her eyes. If she was lucky, she might actually get to wash her hair today. Yesterday Evie, who was four months old today, had woken just as she'd stepped under the water. Not that she really minded. Her tiny daughter was the best thing in her life. The joint best thing, she amended silently.

Tipping her face up to meet the hot spray, she smiled as she thought back to the day of Evie's arrival. Ram had not only turned into a hands-on daddy, he'd practically taken over the entire labour ward.

It had been a small and rare reminder of the old work-hard, play-hard Ram, for nowadays she and Evie were the focus of his passion and devotion. He still loved his job, and the launch had been the most successful in the company's history—but he was happiest when he was at home.

And she was happy too. How could she not be?

She had a handsome, loving husband, a job working with her best friend, and a baby she adored.

Evie was beautiful, a perfect blend of both her parents. She'd inherited her pale skin and loose dark curls from Nola, but she had her father's grey eyes—a fact which, endearingly, Ram pointed out to everyone.

Her skin prickled as the fragrant warm air around her seemed to shift sideways, and then she gasped, her stomach tightening as two warm hands slid around her waist.

'Hi!'

Ram kissed her softly on the neck and, breathing out unsteadily, she leaned back against his warm naked body.

'Hey! That was quick.'

'I haven't done anything yet.'

The teasing note in his voice matched the light, almost tormenting touch of his fingers as they drifted casually over her flat stomach. Turning, she nipped him on the arm, softening it to a kiss as he pulled her closer.

'I meant the interview. I thought you were seeing that super-important woman from the news network?'

Tugging her round to face him, he looked down into her eyes, his mouth curving upwards into one of those sexy smiles she knew would always take her breath away.

'I talked really fast. Besides, I have two far more important women right here!'

'And in about half an hour you'll have three.' She pulled away slightly and smiled up at him.

'Pandora rang. She went shopping yesterday, and she wants to drop off a few things for Evie.'

Ram groaned. 'I presume she went shopping overseas? There can't be anything left in Australia for her to buy.'

Since the night of her anniversary party Pandora had been working hard to rebuild her relationship with her son, and Nola knew that, despite joking about her shopping habits, Ram was touched by his mother's efforts to make amends. She had separated from Guy, and now that they were no longer forced to live together the two of them had begun to enjoy each other's company as friends.

Nola laughed. 'You can talk. Every time you go out of the door you come back with something for me or Evie.'

'She deserves it for being so adorable,' Ram said softly as she glanced down at the beautiful diamond ring he'd given her when Evie was born. 'And you deserve it for giving me such a beautiful daughter.'

And for giving him a life, and a future filled with love.

Gently he ran his hand over her stomach. 'I miss your bump. I feel like I'd just got used to it, and then she was here. Not that I'm complaining.' His eyes softened. 'I can't imagine my life without her *or* you.'

Nola felt a pang of guilt. She knew how much he regretted not being there for the early stages of her pregnancy, for they had no secrets from one another now. That was one of the lessons they'd learnt from their past—to be open with one another.

'I miss it too. But there'll be other bumps.'

'Is that what you want?'

His face had gentled, and she loved him for it, because now everything was about what they *both* wanted.

'It is. It all happened so quickly last time.'

She hesitated, and then, leaning closer, ran her hand slowly over his stomach, her heart stumbling against her ribs as his skin twitched beneath her fingers.

His eyes narrowed, and a curl of heat rose up inside her as he pulled her against his smooth golden body.

'I'm happy to go slowly. On one condition.'

The roughness in his voice made her blood tingle.

'And what's that,' she asked softly.

'That we start right now.'

And, tipping her mouth up to his, he kissed her hungrily.

* * * * *

If you enjoyed
KIDNAPPED FOR THE TYCOON'S BABY
by Louise Fuller
why not explore these other
SECRET HEIRS OF BILLIONAIRES
stories?

THE GREEK'S PLEASURABLE REVENGE
by Andie Brock
THE SECRET KEPT FROM THE GREEK
by Susan Stephens
CARRYING THE SPANIARD'S CHILD
by Jennie Lucas

Available now!

Get 2 Free Books,
Plus 2 Free Gifts—
just for trying the
Reader Service!

♥HARLEQUIN®
Romance

Get 2 Free Books,
Plus 2 Free Gifts—
just for trying the
Reader Service!

Get 2 Free Books,
Plus 2 Free Gifts—
just for trying the Reader Service!

HI17R

Get 2 Free Books,
Plus 2 Free Gifts—
just for trying the Reader Service!

Louise Fuller was a tomboy who hated pink and always wanted to be the prince—not the princess! Now she enjoys creating heroines who aren't pretty pushovers but are strong, believable women. Before writing for Harlequin she studied literature and philosophy at university, and then worked as a reporter for her local newspaper. She lives in Tunbridge Wells with her impossibly handsome husband, Patrick, and their six children.

Books by Louise Fuller

Harlequin Presents

Blackmailed Down the Aisle
Claiming His Wedding Night
A Deal Sealed by Passion
Vows Made in Secret

Visit the Author Profile page at Harlequin.com for more titles.

For Adrian. My brother, and one of the good guys.